geeky f@b 5

Lucy

Zara

Marina

A.J.

Sofia

Hubble

PAPERCUTZ™

THE SMURFS #21

BRINA THE CAT #1

CAT & CAT #1

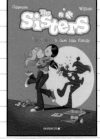

THE SISTERS #1

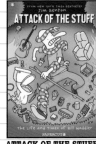

ATTACK OF THE STUFF

SCHOOL FOR EXTRA-
TERRESTRIAL GIRLS

DANCE CLASS 3 IN1

GERONIMO STILTON
RREPORTER #1

THE MYTHICS #1

GUMBY #1

MELOWY #1

BLUEBEARD

THE RED SHOES

THE LITTLE
MERMAID

FUZZY BASEBALL #1

HOTEL
TRANSYLVANIA #1

THE LOUD HOUSE #1

MANOSAURS #1

THE ONLY LIVING
BOY #5

ONLY LIVING GIRL #1

MORE GREAT GRAPHIC NOVEL SERIES AVAILABLE FROM

PAPERCUTZ™

papercutz.com

All available where ebooks are sold.

School For Extraterrestrial Girls © 2020 Jeremy Whitley and Jamie Noguchi; Geronimo Stilton Reporter, Melowy © 2020 Atlantyca S.p.A; The Little Mermaid and The Red Shoes © 2018 Metaphrog; Fuzzy Baseball © 2020 by John Steven Gurney; The Loud House © 2020 Viacom International Inc.; Manosaurs ©2020 Stuart Fischer and Papercutz; The Only Living Boy, The Only Living Girl © 2020 Bottled Lightning LLC.; GUMBY ©2020 Prema Toy Co., Inc.; The Sisters, Cat & Cat, Dance Class © 2020 BAMBOO ÉDITION; Attack of the Stuff © 2020 Jim Benton Arts; Brina the Cat © 2020 TUNUÉ (Tunué s.r.l.) - Giorgio Salati and Christian Cornia.

geeky f@b 5 ®

#4 "Food Fight for Fiona"

LUCY & LIZ LAREAU — Writers
RYAN JAMPOLE — Artist

PAPERCUTZ™
NEW YORK

geeky f@b 5 ®

#4 "Food Fight for Fiona"

LUCY & LIZ LAREAU—Writers
RYAN JAMPOLE—Artist and Cover Artist
LAURIE E. SMITH—Colorist
WILSON RAMOS JR.—Letterer
MANOSAUR MARTIN—Production
JEFF WHITMAN—Managing Editor
JIM SALICRUP
Editor-in-Chief

Copyright ©2020 by Geeky Fab Five, Inc. All rights reserved.
"The Geeky Fab Five" and "Five Girls. Big Problems. One School" are
registered trademarks of Geeky Fab Five, Inc.
All other material © 2020 Papercutz.
papercutz.com
geekyfabfive.com

Special thanks to the Illinois Agriculture in the Classroom organization
for their guidance with the GF5's visit to the farm.

Hardcover ISBN 978-1-5458-0346-2
Paperback ISBN 978-1-5458-0364-6

Printed in China
September 2020

Papercutz books may be purchased for business or promotional use.
For information on bulk purchases, please contact Macmillan Corporate
and Premium Sales Department at (800) 221-7945 x5442.

Distributed by Macmillan
First Printing

In memory of Tom Kitten, 2009-2020, whose stubborn independence and infinite kitty love inspired our creation of Hubble. We love you, Tommy. –Lucy & Liz

Teacher's Guide available at:
http://papercutz.com/educator-resources-papercutz

CHAPTER ONE: A SPARKLY BLAST

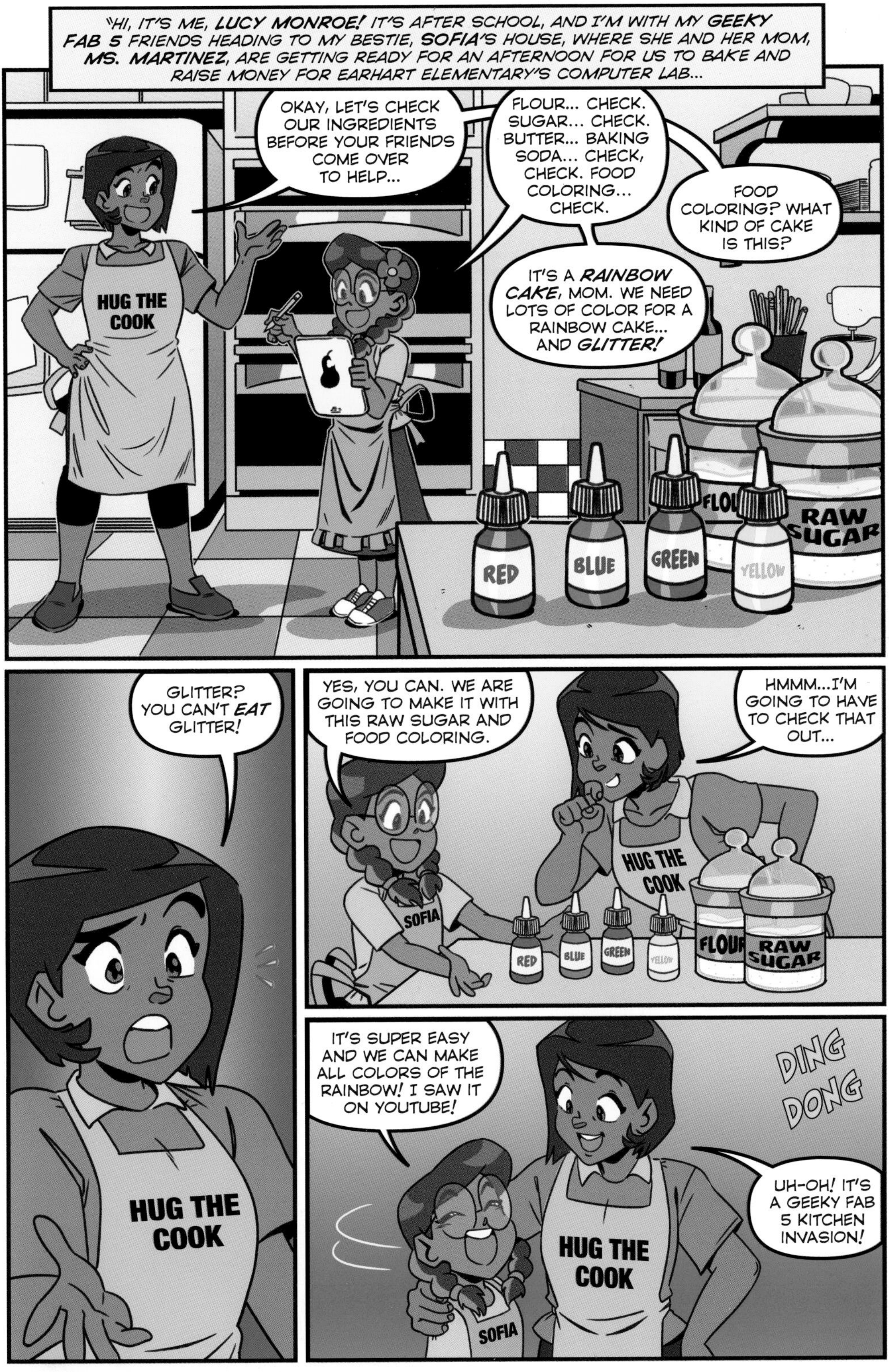
"HI, IT'S ME, LUCY MONROE! IT'S AFTER SCHOOL, AND I'M WITH MY GEEKY FAB 5 FRIENDS HEADING TO MY BESTIE, SOFIA'S HOUSE, WHERE SHE AND HER MOM, MS. MARTINEZ, ARE GETTING READY FOR AN AFTERNOON FOR US TO BAKE AND RAISE MONEY FOR EARHART ELEMENTARY'S COMPUTER LAB...
OKAY, LET'S CHECK OUR INGREDIENTS BEFORE YOUR FRIENDS COME OVER TO HELP...
FLOUR... CHECK. SUGAR... CHECK. BUTTER... BAKING SODA... CHECK, CHECK. FOOD COLORING... CHECK.
FOOD COLORING? WHAT KIND OF CAKE IS THIS?
IT'S A RAINBOW CAKE, MOM. WE NEED LOTS OF COLOR FOR A RAINBOW CAKE... AND GLITTER!
HUG THE COOK
RED
BLUE
GREEN
YELLOW
FLOUR
RAW SUGAR
GLITTER? YOU CAN'T EAT GLITTER!
HUG THE COOK
YES, YOU CAN. WE ARE GOING TO MAKE IT WITH THIS RAW SUGAR AND FOOD COLORING.
HMMM...I'M GOING TO HAVE TO CHECK THAT OUT...
SOFIA
HUG THE COOK
IT'S SUPER EASY AND WE CAN MAKE ALL COLORS OF THE RAINBOW! I SAW IT ON YOUTUBE!
DING DONG
UH-OH! IT'S A GEEKY FAB 5 KITCHEN INVASION!
HUG THE COOK
SOFIA

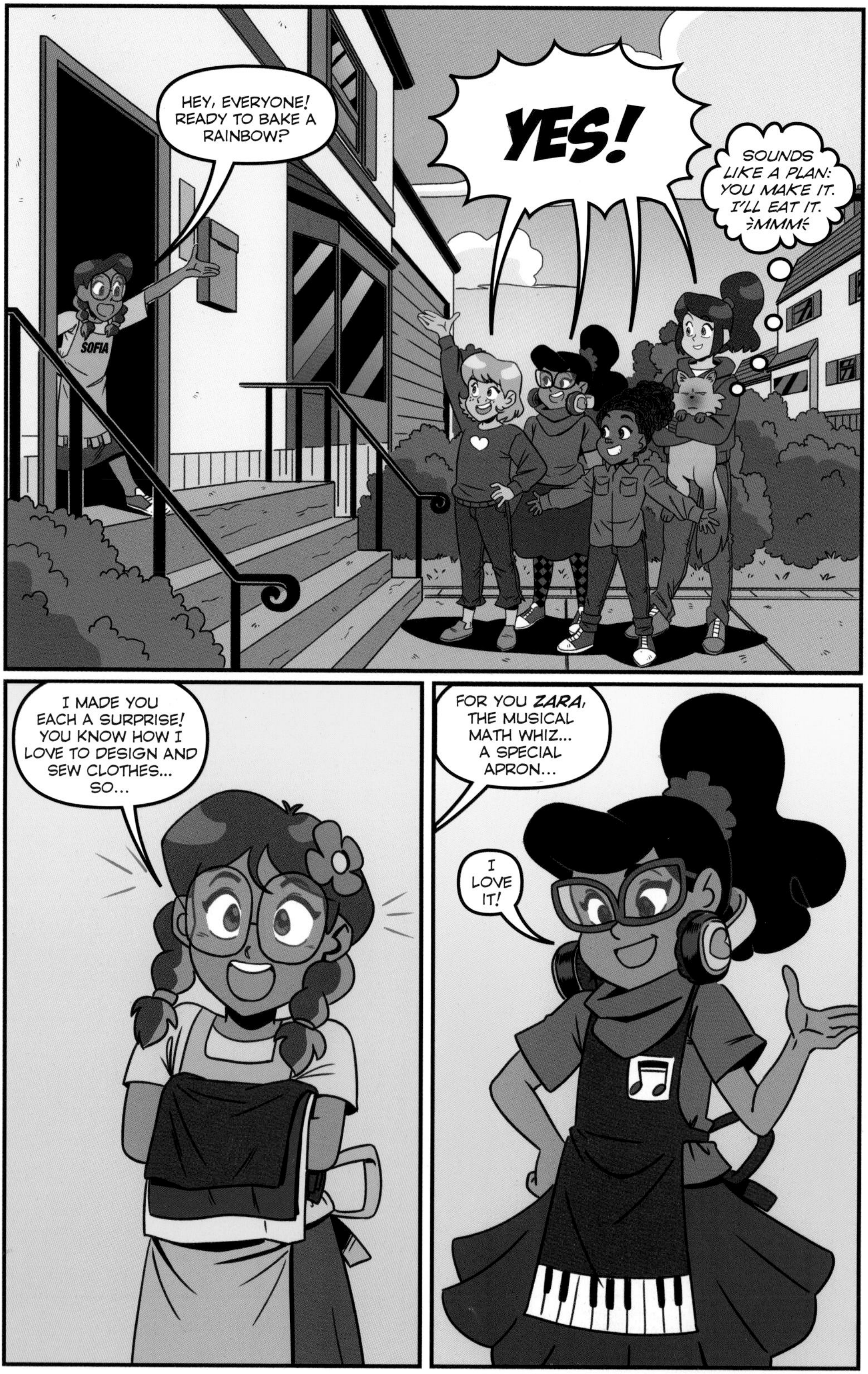
HEY, EVERYONE! READY TO BAKE A RAINBOW?
YES!
SOUNDS LIKE A PLAN: YOU MAKE IT. I'LL EAT IT. MMM
SOFIA
I MADE YOU EACH A SURPRISE! YOU KNOW HOW I LOVE TO DESIGN AND SEW CLOTHES... SO...
FOR YOU ZARA, THE MUSICAL MATH WHIZ... A SPECIAL APRON...
I LOVE IT!

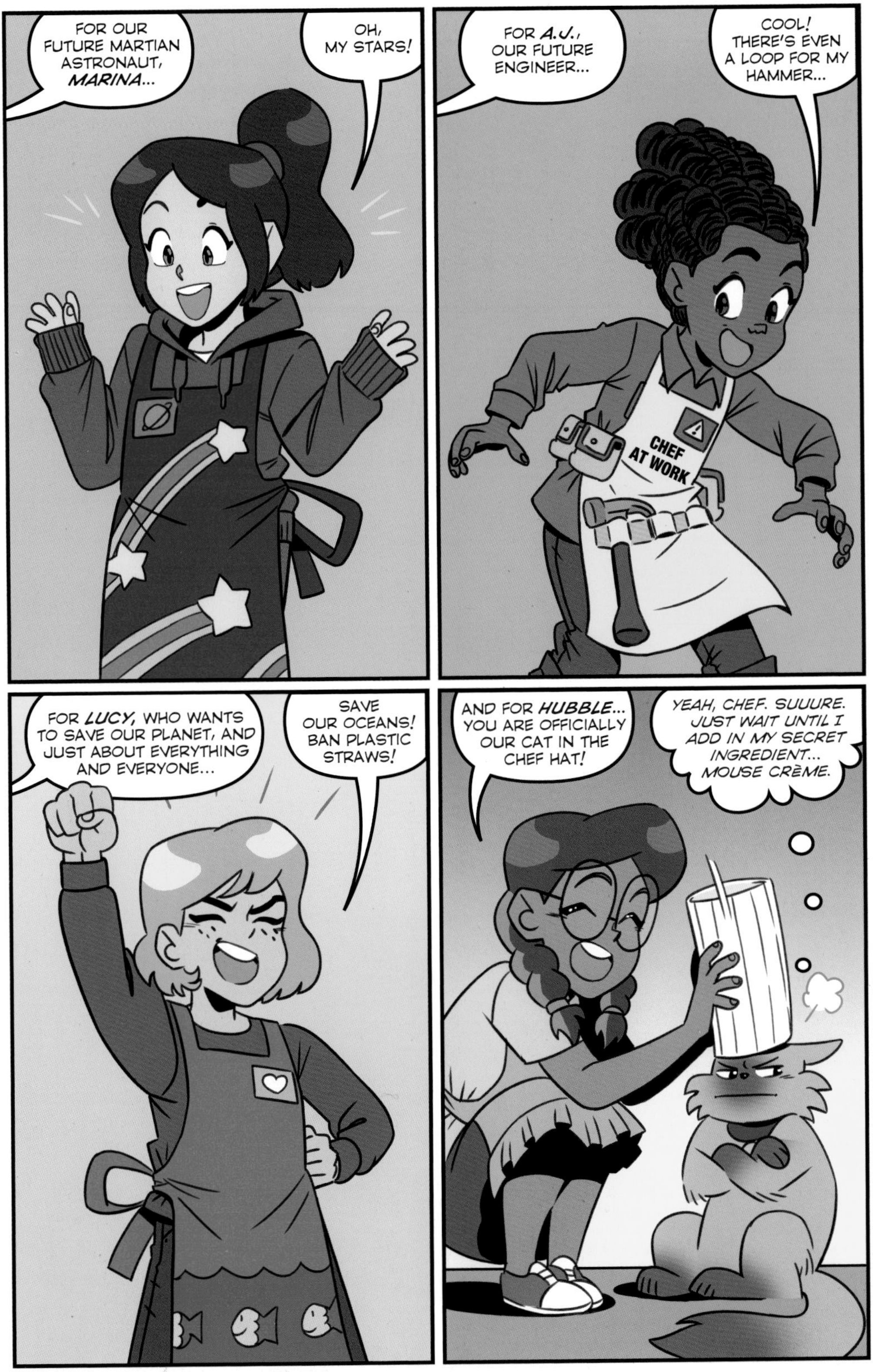
FOR OUR FUTURE MARTIAN ASTRONAUT, MARINA...
OH, MY STARS!
FOR A.J., OUR FUTURE ENGINEER...
COOL! THERE'S EVEN A LOOP FOR MY HAMMER...
CHEF AT WORK
FOR LUCY, WHO WANTS TO SAVE OUR PLANET, AND JUST ABOUT EVERYTHING AND EVERYONE...
SAVE OUR OCEANS! BAN PLASTIC STRAWS!
AND FOR HUBBLE... YOU ARE OFFICIALLY OUR CAT IN THE CHEF HAT!
YEAH, CHEF. SUUURE. JUST WAIT UNTIL I ADD IN MY SECRET INGREDIENT... MOUSE CRÈME.

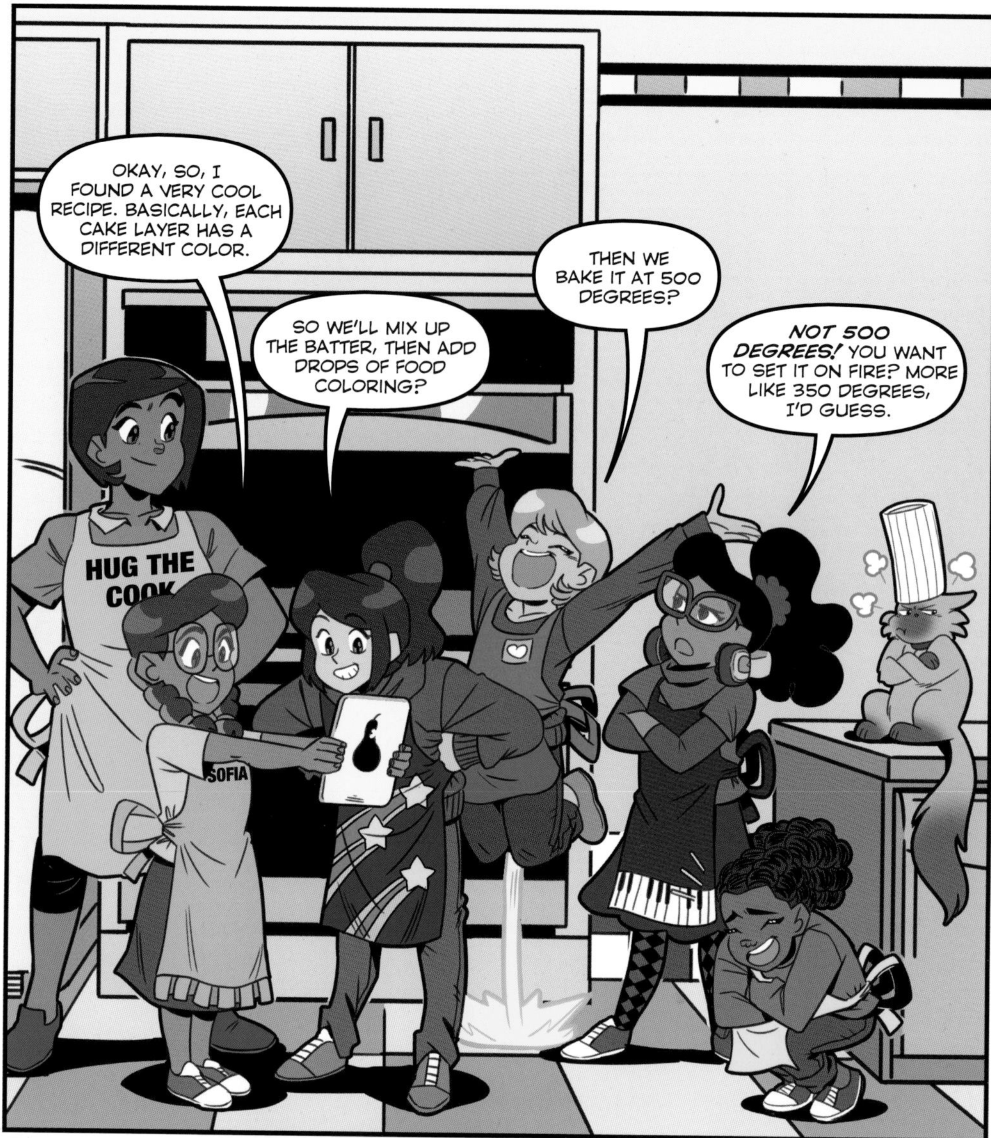
OKAY, SO, I FOUND A VERY COOL RECIPE. BASICALLY, EACH CAKE LAYER HAS A DIFFERENT COLOR.
HUG THE COOK
SO WE'LL MIX UP THE BATTER, THEN ADD DROPS OF FOOD COLORING?
THEN WE BAKE IT AT 500 DEGREES?
NOT 500 DEGREES! YOU WANT TO SET IT ON FIRE? MORE LIKE 350 DEGREES, I'D GUESS.
SOFIA

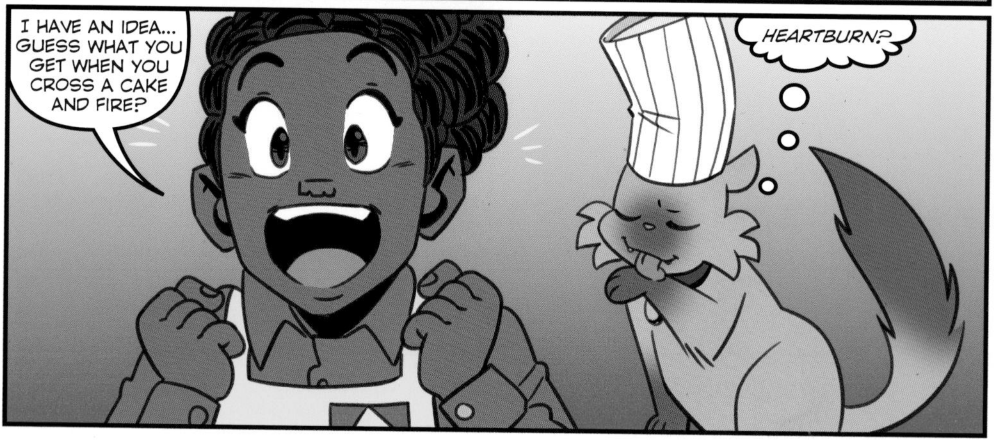
I HAVE AN IDEA... GUESS WHAT YOU GET WHEN YOU CROSS A CAKE AND FIRE?
HEARTBURN?

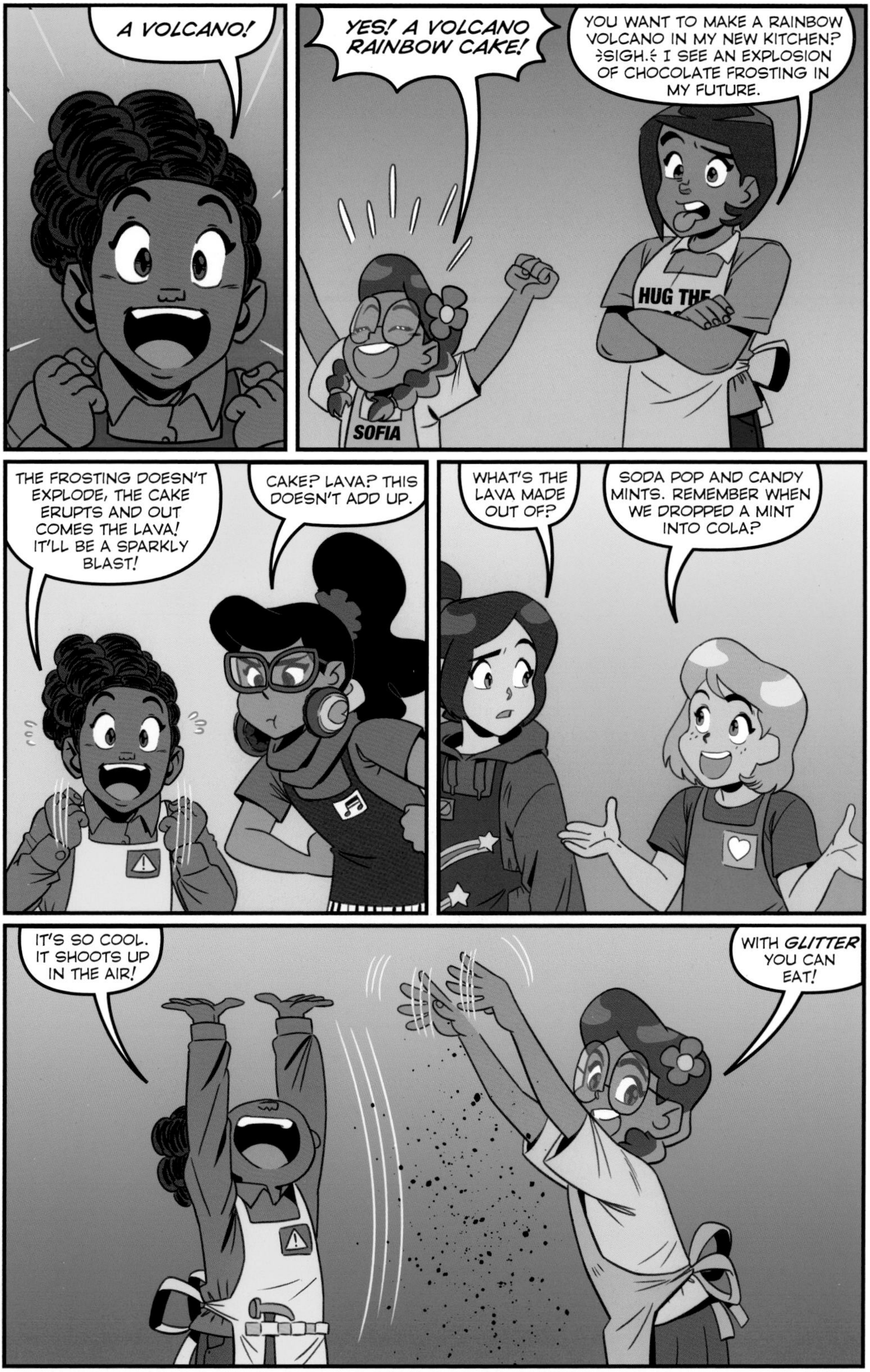
A VOLCANO!
YES! A VOLCANO RAINBOW CAKE!
YOU WANT TO MAKE A RAINBOW VOLCANO IN MY NEW KITCHEN? *SIGH.* I SEE AN EXPLOSION OF CHOCOLATE FROSTING IN MY FUTURE.
HUG THE
SOFIA
THE FROSTING DOESN'T EXPLODE, THE CAKE ERUPTS AND OUT COMES THE LAVA! IT'LL BE A SPARKLY BLAST!
CAKE? LAVA? THIS DOESN'T ADD UP.
WHAT'S THE LAVA MADE OUT OF?
SODA POP AND CANDY MINTS. REMEMBER WHEN WE DROPPED A MINT INTO COLA?
IT'S SO COOL. IT SHOOTS UP IN THE AIR!
WITH *GLITTER* YOU CAN EAT!

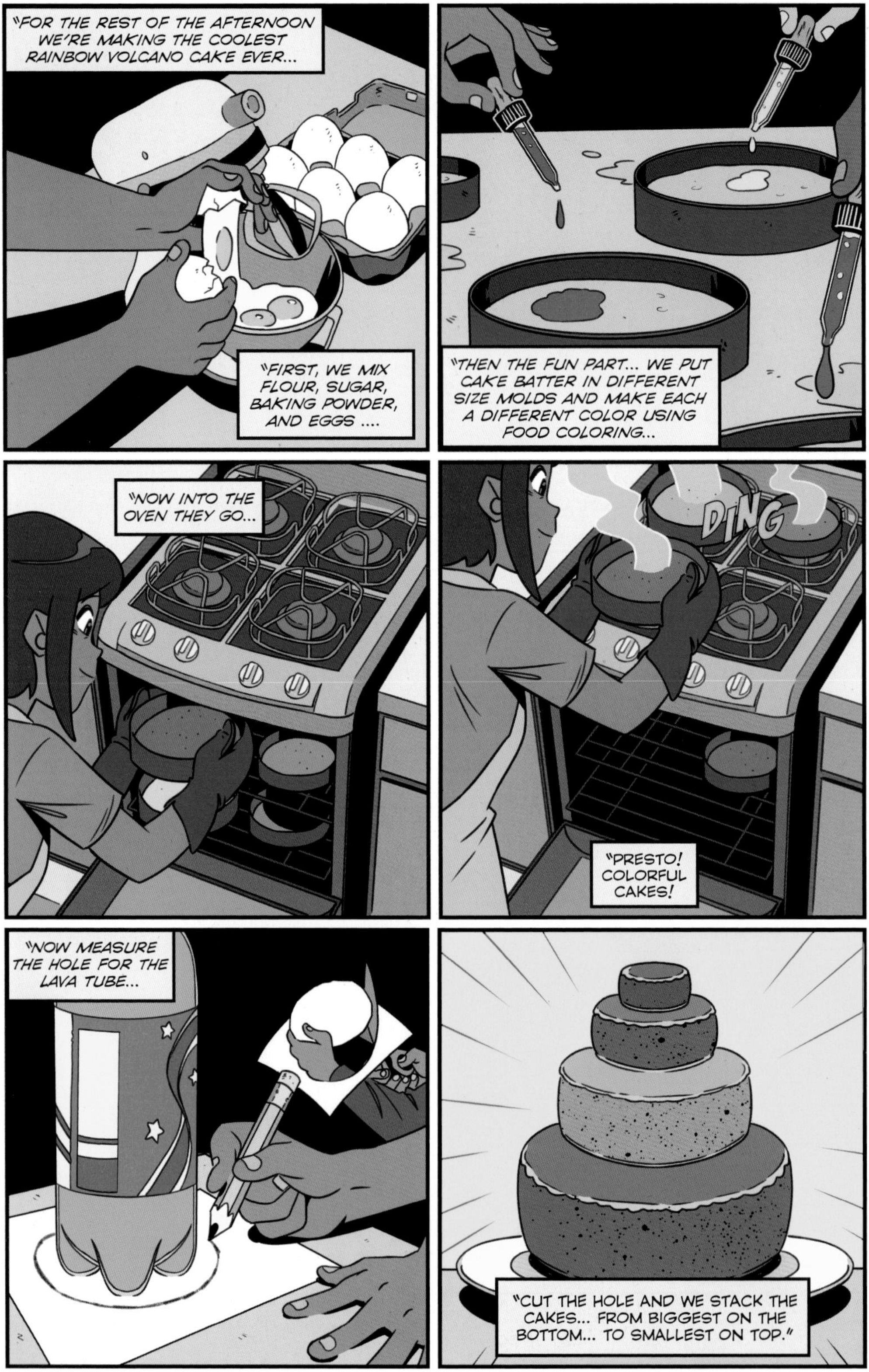
"FOR THE REST OF THE AFTERNOON WE'RE MAKING THE COOLEST RAINBOW VOLCANO CAKE EVER...
"FIRST, WE MIX FLOUR, SUGAR, BAKING POWDER, AND EGGS ....
"THEN THE FUN PART... WE PUT CAKE BATTER IN DIFFERENT SIZE MOLDS AND MAKE EACH A DIFFERENT COLOR USING FOOD COLORING...
"NOW INTO THE OVEN THEY GO...
DING
"PRESTO! COLORFUL CAKES!
"NOW MEASURE THE HOLE FOR THE LAVA TUBE...
"CUT THE HOLE AND WE STACK THE CAKES... FROM BIGGEST ON THE BOTTOM... TO SMALLEST ON TOP."

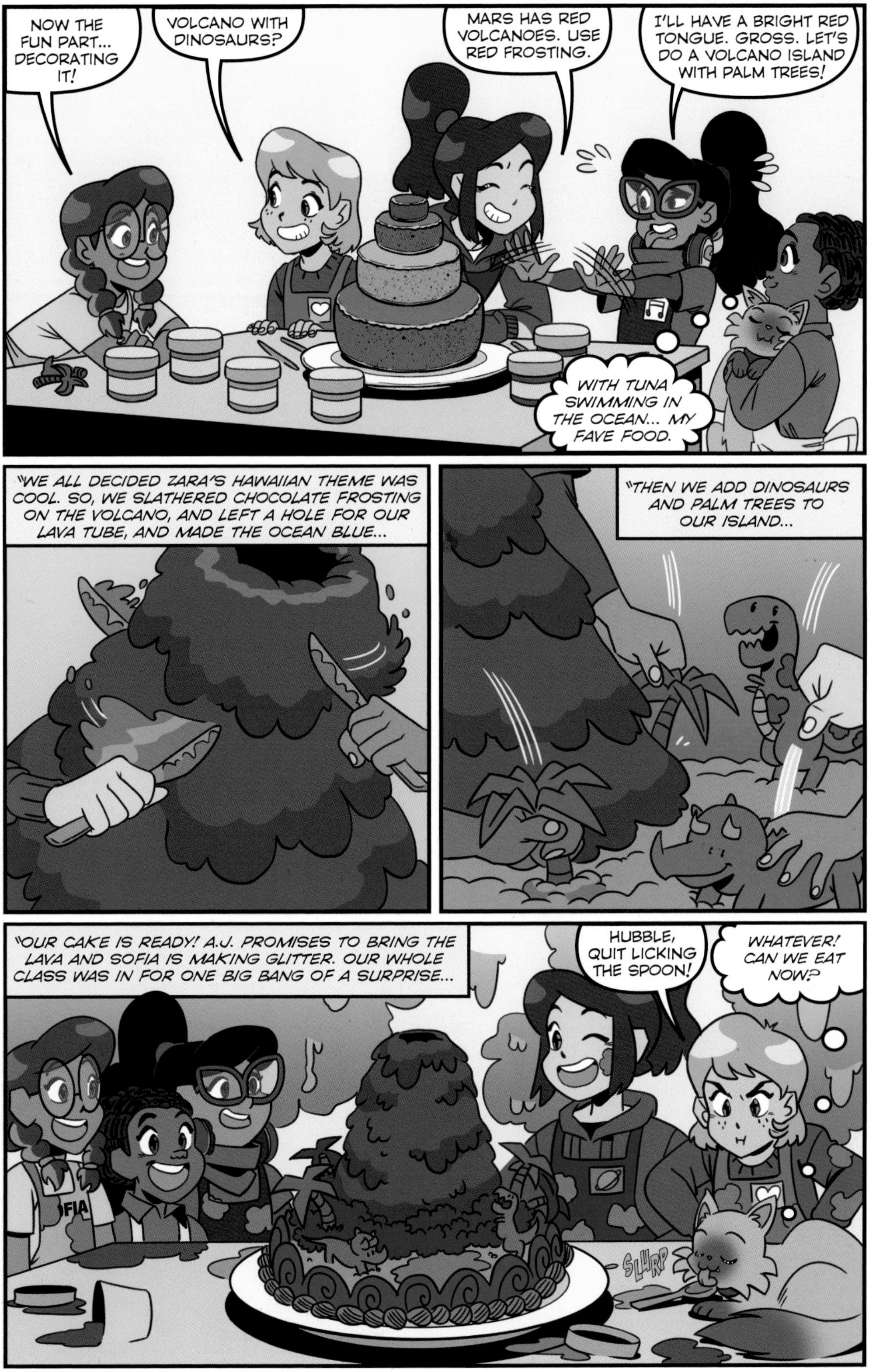
NOW THE FUN PART... DECORATING IT!
VOLCANO WITH DINOSAURS?
MARS HAS RED VOLCANOES. USE RED FROSTING.
I'LL HAVE A BRIGHT RED TONGUE. GROSS. LET'S DO A VOLCANO ISLAND WITH PALM TREES!
WITH TUNA SWIMMING IN THE OCEAN... MY FAVE FOOD.
"WE ALL DECIDED ZARA'S HAWAIIAN THEME WAS COOL. SO, WE SLATHERED CHOCOLATE FROSTING ON THE VOLCANO, AND LEFT A HOLE FOR OUR LAVA TUBE, AND MADE THE OCEAN BLUE...
"THEN WE ADD DINOSAURS AND PALM TREES TO OUR ISLAND...
"OUR CAKE IS READY! A.J. PROMISES TO BRING THE LAVA AND SOFIA IS MAKING GLITTER. OUR WHOLE CLASS WAS IN FOR ONE BIG BANG OF A SURPRISE...
HUBBLE, QUIT LICKING THE SPOON!
WHATEVER! CAN WE EAT NOW?
SOFIA
SLURP

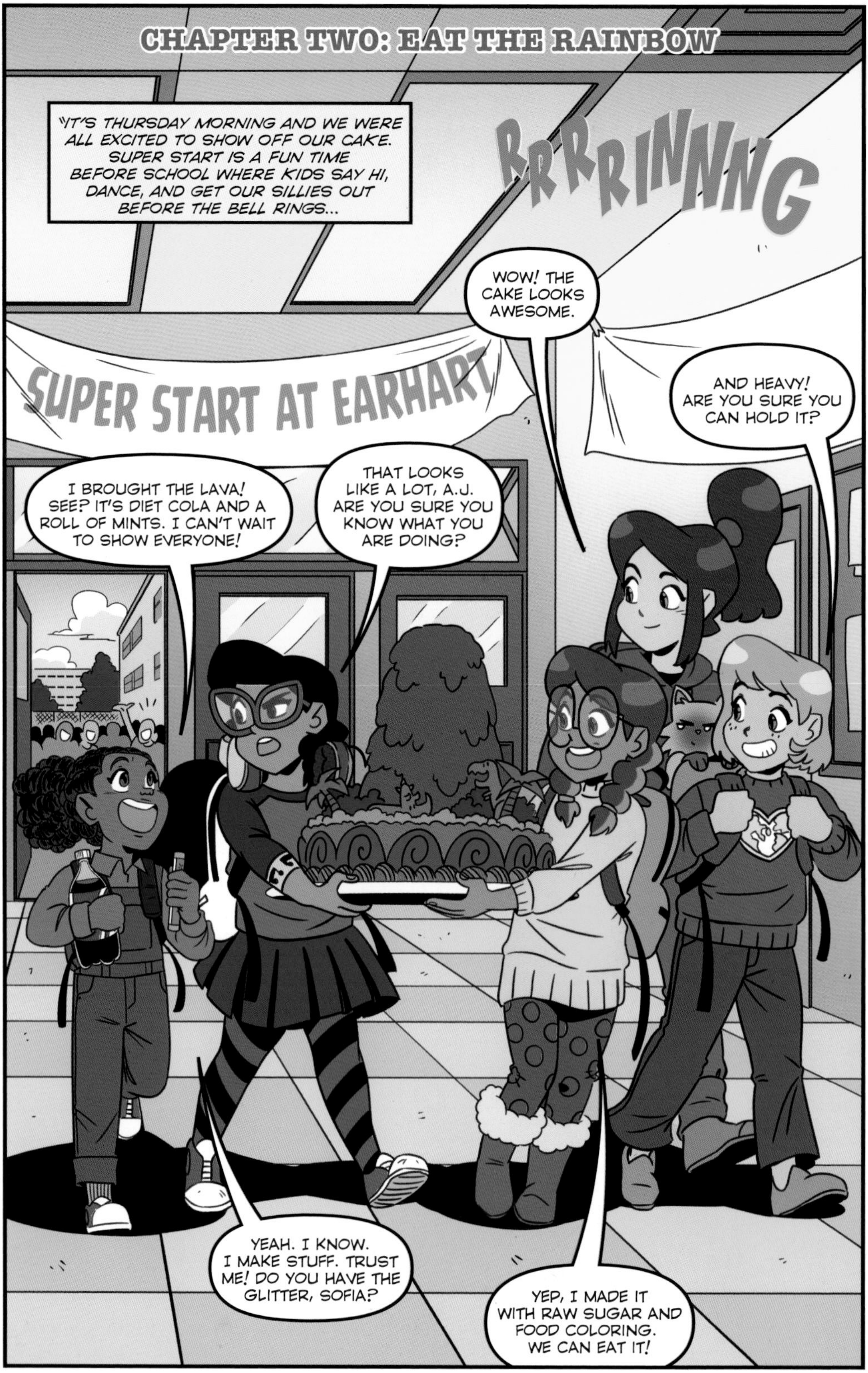
CHAPTER TWO: EAT THE RAINBOW
"IT'S THURSDAY MORNING AND WE WERE ALL EXCITED TO SHOW OFF OUR CAKE. SUPER START IS A FUN TIME BEFORE SCHOOL WHERE KIDS SAY HI, DANCE, AND GET OUR SILLIES OUT BEFORE THE BELL RINGS...
BRRRINNNG
WOW! THE CAKE LOOKS AWESOME.
SUPER START AT EARHART
AND HEAVY! ARE YOU SURE YOU CAN HOLD IT?
I BROUGHT THE LAVA! SEE? IT'S DIET COLA AND A ROLL OF MINTS. I CAN'T WAIT TO SHOW EVERYONE!
THAT LOOKS LIKE A LOT, A.J. ARE YOU SURE YOU KNOW WHAT YOU ARE DOING?
YEAH. I KNOW. I MAKE STUFF. TRUST ME! DO YOU HAVE THE GLITTER, SOFIA?
YEP, I MADE IT WITH RAW SUGAR AND FOOD COLORING. WE CAN EAT IT!

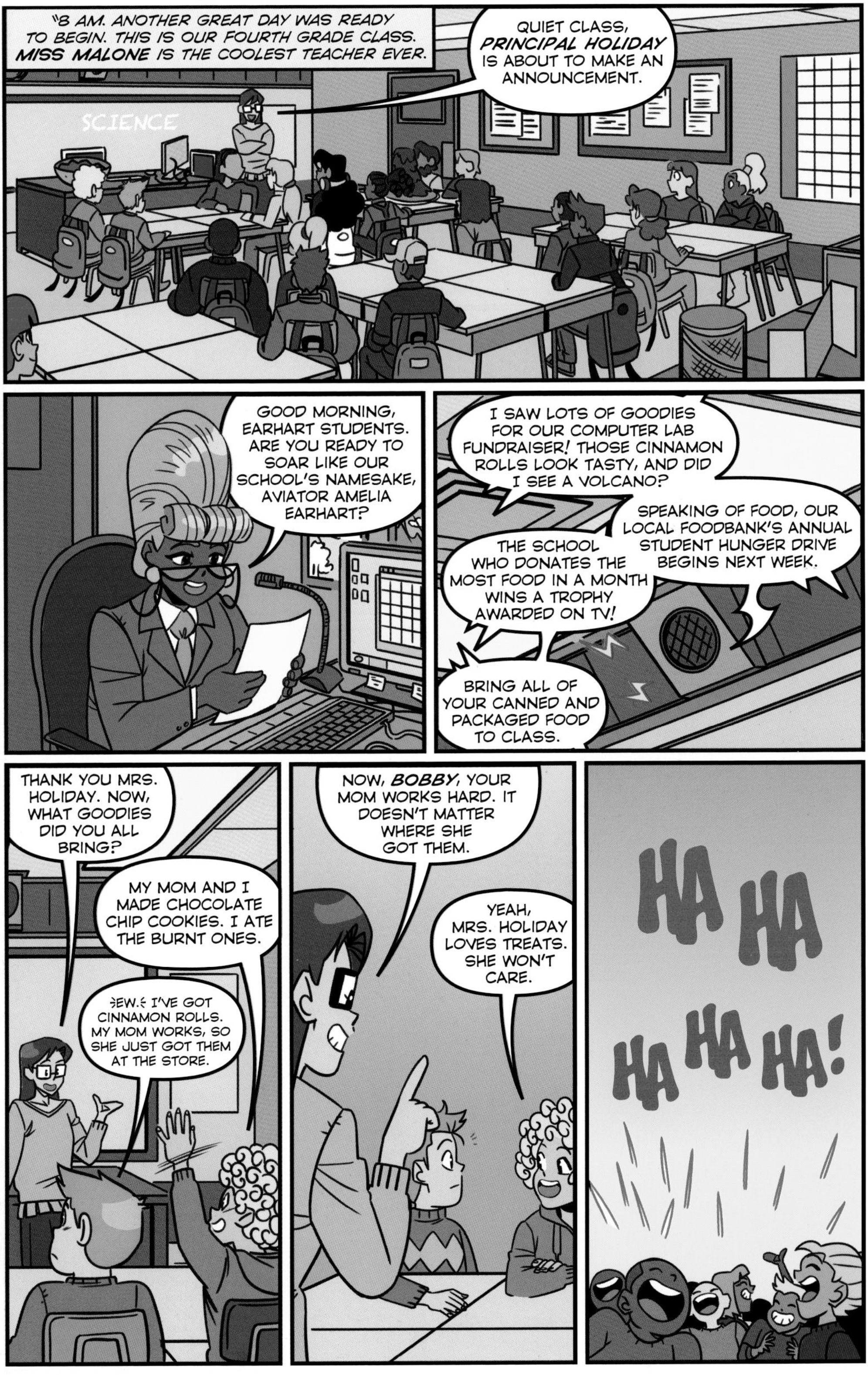
"8 AM. ANOTHER GREAT DAY WAS READY TO BEGIN. THIS IS OUR FOURTH GRADE CLASS. MISS MALONE IS THE COOLEST TEACHER EVER.
QUIET CLASS, PRINCIPAL HOLIDAY IS ABOUT TO MAKE AN ANNOUNCEMENT.
SCIENCE
GOOD MORNING, EARHART STUDENTS. ARE YOU READY TO SOAR LIKE OUR SCHOOL'S NAMESAKE, AVIATOR AMELIA EARHART?
I SAW LOTS OF GOODIES FOR OUR COMPUTER LAB FUNDRAISER! THOSE CINNAMON ROLLS LOOK TASTY, AND DID I SEE A VOLCANO?
SPEAKING OF FOOD, OUR LOCAL FOODBANK'S ANNUAL STUDENT HUNGER DRIVE BEGINS NEXT WEEK.
THE SCHOOL WHO DONATES THE MOST FOOD IN A MONTH WINS A TROPHY AWARDED ON TV!
BRING ALL OF YOUR CANNED AND PACKAGED FOOD TO CLASS.
THANK YOU MRS. HOLIDAY. NOW, WHAT GOODIES DID YOU ALL BRING?
MY MOM AND I MADE CHOCOLATE CHIP COOKIES. I ATE THE BURNT ONES.
EW. I'VE GOT CINNAMON ROLLS. MY MOM WORKS, SO SHE JUST GOT THEM AT THE STORE.
NOW, BOBBY, YOUR MOM WORKS HARD. IT DOESN'T MATTER WHERE SHE GOT THEM.
YEAH, MRS. HOLIDAY LOVES TREATS. SHE WON'T CARE.
HA HA
HA HA HA HA!

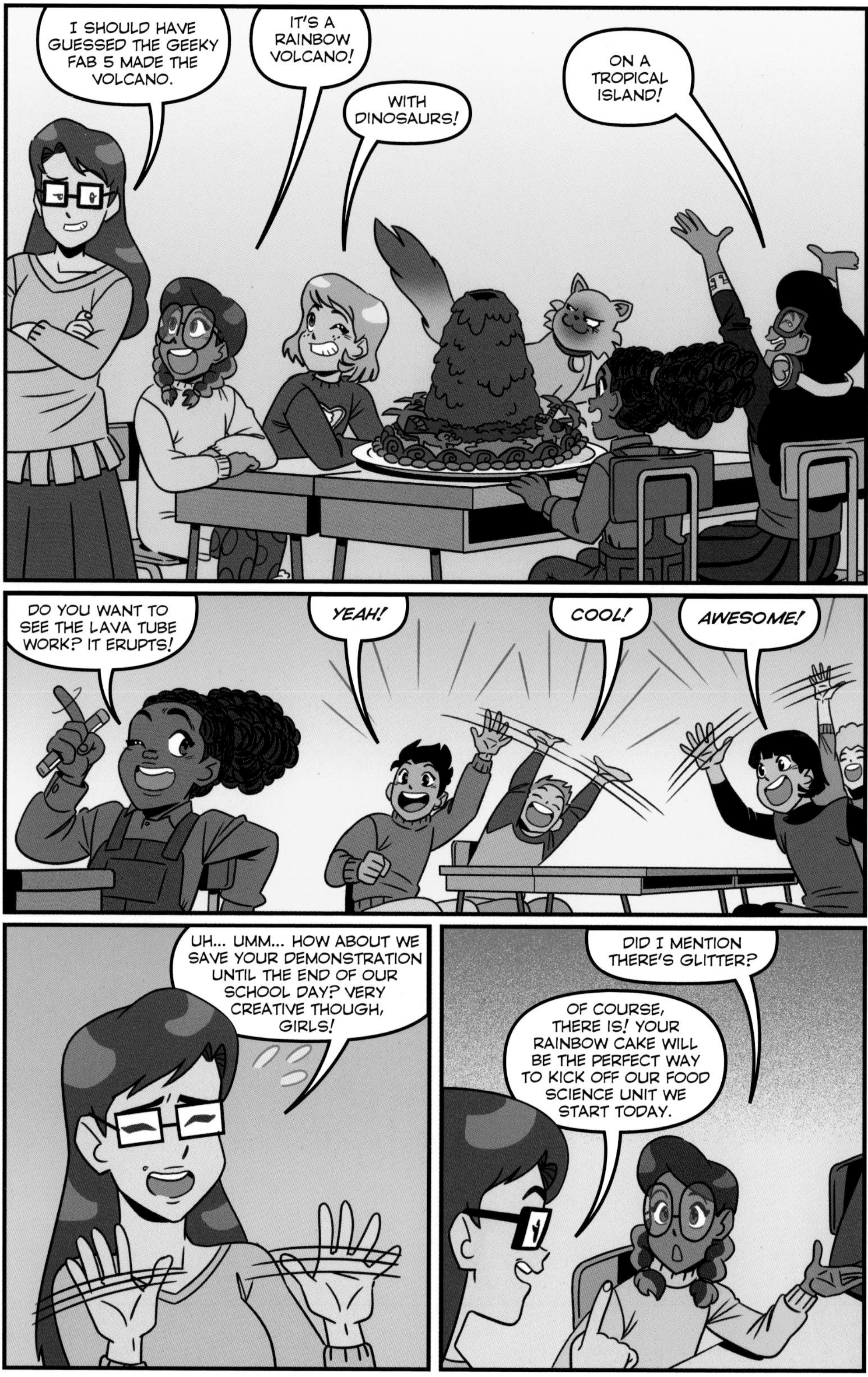
I SHOULD HAVE GUESSED THE GEEKY FAB 5 MADE THE VOLCANO.
IT'S A RAINBOW VOLCANO!
WITH DINOSAURS!
ON A TROPICAL ISLAND!
DO YOU WANT TO SEE THE LAVA TUBE WORK? IT ERUPTS!
YEAH!
COOL!
AWESOME!
UH... UMM... HOW ABOUT WE SAVE YOUR DEMONSTRATION UNTIL THE END OF OUR SCHOOL DAY? VERY CREATIVE THOUGH, GIRLS!
DID I MENTION THERE'S GLITTER?
OF COURSE, THERE IS! YOUR RAINBOW CAKE WILL BE THE PERFECT WAY TO KICK OFF OUR FOOD SCIENCE UNIT WE START TODAY.

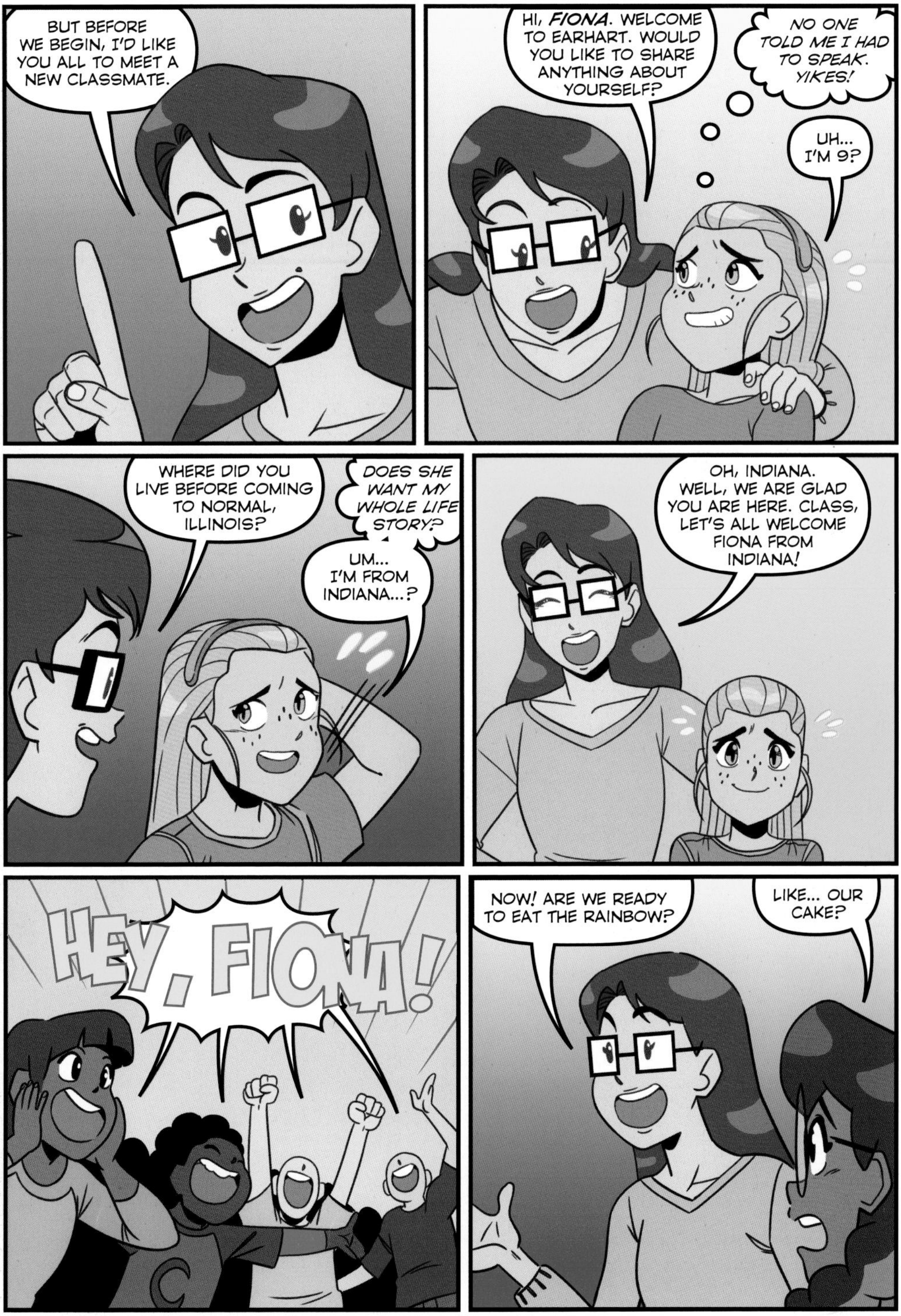
BUT BEFORE WE BEGIN, I'D LIKE YOU ALL TO MEET A NEW CLASSMATE.
HI, *FIONA*. WELCOME TO EARHART. WOULD YOU LIKE TO SHARE ANYTHING ABOUT YOURSELF?
NO ONE TOLD ME I HAD TO SPEAK. YIKES!
UH... I'M 9?
WHERE DID YOU LIVE BEFORE COMING TO NORMAL, ILLINOIS?
DOES SHE WANT MY WHOLE LIFE STORY?
UM... I'M FROM INDIANA...?
OH, INDIANA. WELL, WE ARE GLAD YOU ARE HERE. CLASS, LET'S ALL WELCOME FIONA FROM INDIANA!
HEY, FIONA!
NOW! ARE WE READY TO EAT THE RAINBOW?
LIKE... OUR CAKE?

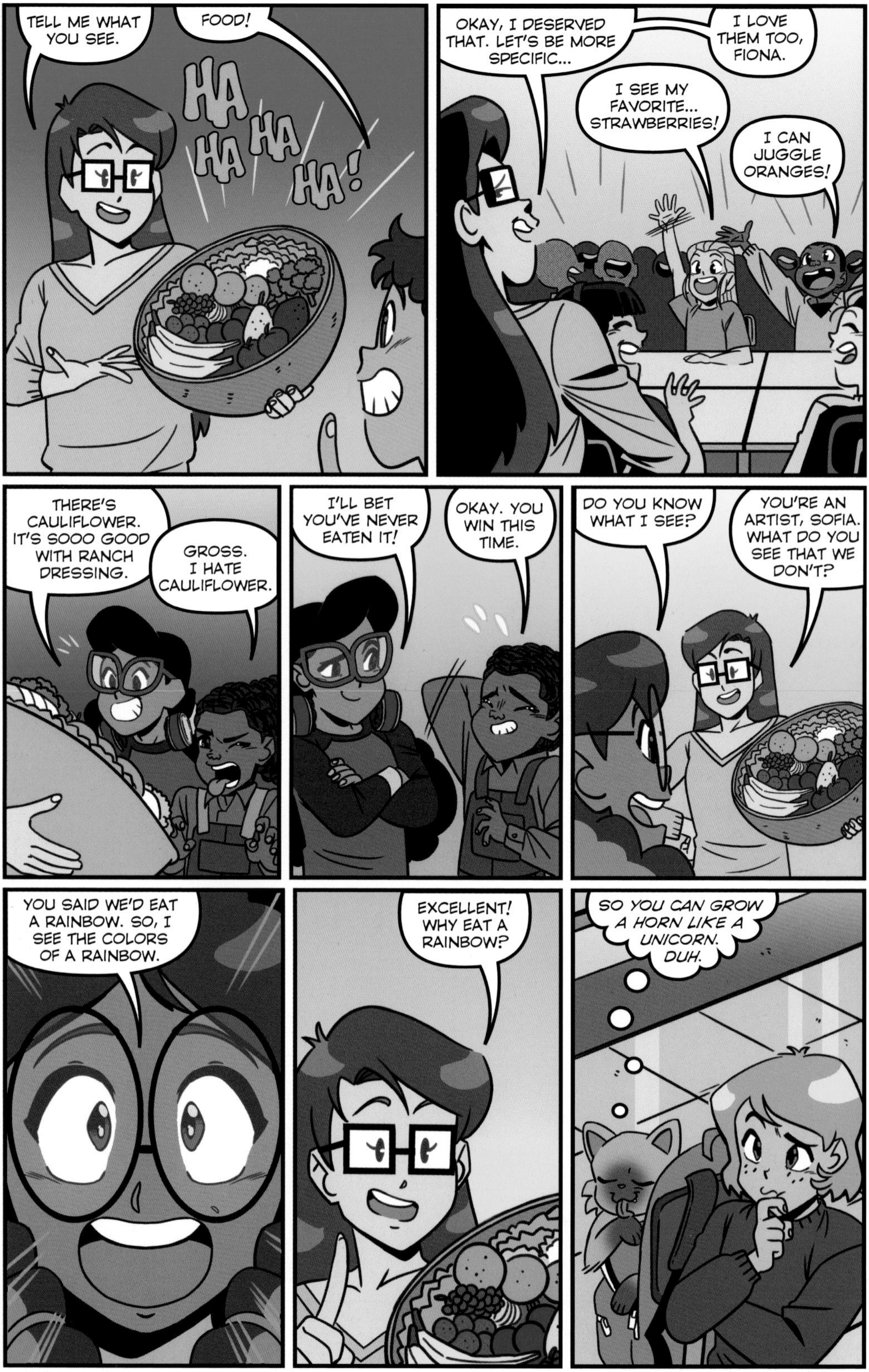
TELL ME WHAT YOU SEE.
FOOD!
HA HA HA HA HA!
OKAY, I DESERVED THAT. LET'S BE MORE SPECIFIC...
I LOVE THEM TOO, FIONA.
I SEE MY FAVORITE... STRAWBERRIES!
I CAN JUGGLE ORANGES!
THERE'S CAULIFLOWER. IT'S SOOO GOOD WITH RANCH DRESSING.
GROSS. I HATE CAULIFLOWER.
I'LL BET YOU'VE NEVER EATEN IT!
OKAY. YOU WIN THIS TIME.
DO YOU KNOW WHAT I SEE?
YOU'RE AN ARTIST, SOFIA. WHAT DO YOU SEE THAT WE DON'T?
YOU SAID WE'D EAT A RAINBOW. SO, I SEE THE COLORS OF A RAINBOW.
EXCELLENT! WHY EAT A RAINBOW?
SO YOU CAN GROW A HORN LIKE A UNICORN. DUH.

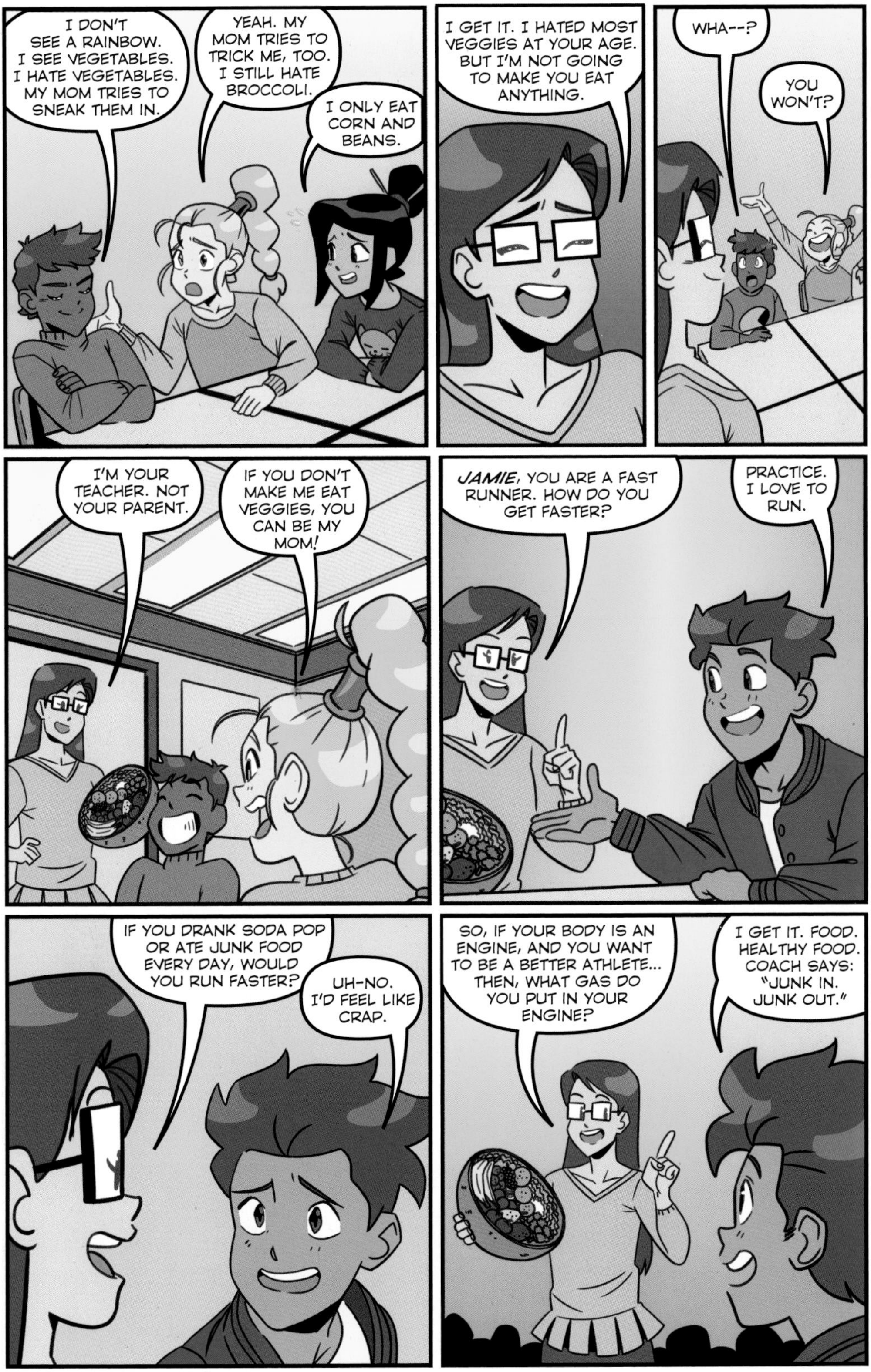
I DON'T SEE A RAINBOW. I SEE VEGETABLES. I HATE VEGETABLES. MY MOM TRIES TO SNEAK THEM IN.
YEAH. MY MOM TRIES TO TRICK ME, TOO. I STILL HATE BROCCOLI.
I ONLY EAT CORN AND BEANS.
I GET IT. I HATED MOST VEGGIES AT YOUR AGE. BUT I'M NOT GOING TO MAKE YOU EAT ANYTHING.
WHA--?
YOU WON'T?
I'M YOUR TEACHER. NOT YOUR PARENT.
IF YOU DON'T MAKE ME EAT VEGGIES, YOU CAN BE MY MOM!
JAMIE, YOU ARE A FAST RUNNER. HOW DO YOU GET FASTER?
PRACTICE. I LOVE TO RUN.
IF YOU DRANK SODA POP OR ATE JUNK FOOD EVERY DAY, WOULD YOU RUN FASTER?
UH-NO. I'D FEEL LIKE CRAP.
SO, IF YOUR BODY IS AN ENGINE, AND YOU WANT TO BE A BETTER ATHLETE... THEN, WHAT GAS DO YOU PUT IN YOUR ENGINE?
I GET IT. FOOD. HEALTHY FOOD. COACH SAYS: "JUNK IN. JUNK OUT."

YELLOW FOODS, SUCH AS BANANAS, ARE GOOD FOR YOUR HEART, EYES, AND SKIN.

WHITE FOODS, SUCH AS CAULIFLOWER, HELP YOUR BLOOD CIRCULATE THROUGHOUT YOUR BODY.

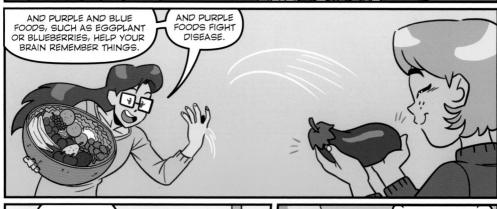

AND PURPLE AND BLUE FOODS, SUCH AS EGGPLANT OR BLUEBERRIES, HELP YOUR BRAIN REMEMBER THINGS.

AND PURPLE FOODS FIGHT DISEASE.

FOOD IS GAS FOR YOUR ENGINES!

SPEAKING OF GAS... I HOPE IT'S BEANIE WEANIES FOR LUNCH. MY TUMMY IS RUMBLY...

GROW

18

CHAPTER THREE: HUNGER AT HOME

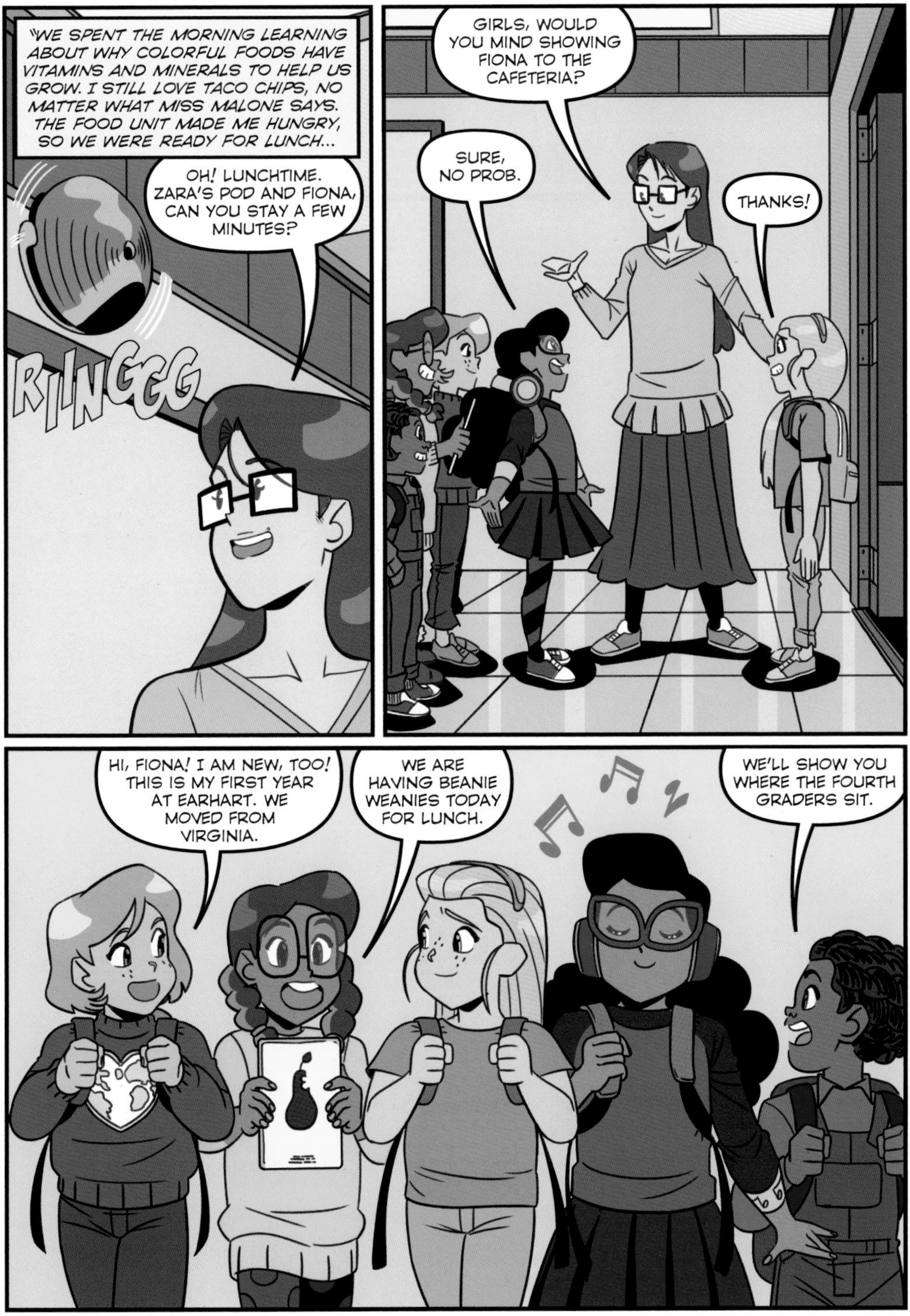

"WE SPENT THE MORNING LEARNING ABOUT WHY COLORFUL FOODS HAVE VITAMINS AND MINERALS TO HELP US GROW. I STILL LOVE TACO CHIPS, NO MATTER WHAT MISS MALONE SAYS. THE FOOD UNIT MADE ME HUNGRY, SO WE WERE READY FOR LUNCH...
OH! LUNCHTIME. ZARA'S POD AND FIONA, CAN YOU STAY A FEW MINUTES?
RIINGGG
GIRLS, WOULD YOU MIND SHOWING FIONA TO THE CAFETERIA?
SURE, NO PROB.
THANKS!
HI, FIONA! I AM NEW, TOO! THIS IS MY FIRST YEAR AT EARHART. WE MOVED FROM VIRGINIA.
WE ARE HAVING BEANIE WEANIES TODAY FOR LUNCH.
WE'LL SHOW YOU WHERE THE FOURTH GRADERS SIT.

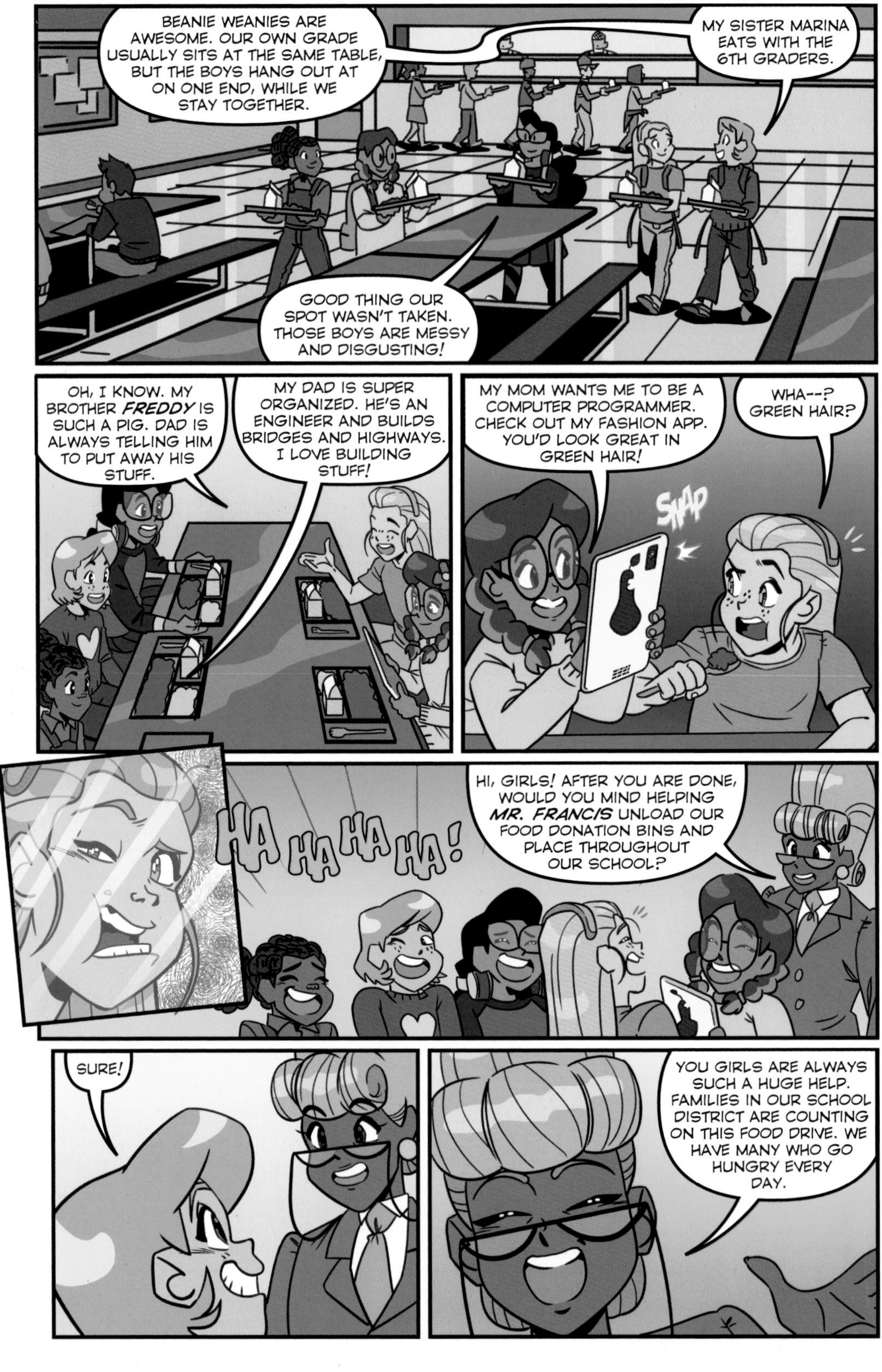
BEANIE WEANIES ARE AWESOME. OUR OWN GRADE USUALLY SITS AT THE SAME TABLE, BUT THE BOYS HANG OUT AT ON ONE END, WHILE WE STAY TOGETHER.
MY SISTER MARINA EATS WITH THE 6TH GRADERS.
GOOD THING OUR SPOT WASN'T TAKEN. THOSE BOYS ARE MESSY AND DISGUSTING!
OH, I KNOW. MY BROTHER FREDDY IS SUCH A PIG. DAD IS ALWAYS TELLING HIM TO PUT AWAY HIS STUFF.
MY DAD IS SUPER ORGANIZED. HE'S AN ENGINEER AND BUILDS BRIDGES AND HIGHWAYS. I LOVE BUILDING STUFF!
MY MOM WANTS ME TO BE A COMPUTER PROGRAMMER. CHECK OUT MY FASHION APP. YOU'D LOOK GREAT IN GREEN HAIR!
WHA--? GREEN HAIR?
SNAP
HA HA HA HA!
HI, GIRLS! AFTER YOU ARE DONE, WOULD YOU MIND HELPING MR. FRANCIS UNLOAD OUR FOOD DONATION BINS AND PLACE THROUGHOUT OUR SCHOOL?
SURE!
YOU GIRLS ARE ALWAYS SUCH A HUGE HELP. FAMILIES IN OUR SCHOOL DISTRICT ARE COUNTING ON THIS FOOD DRIVE. WE HAVE MANY WHO GO HUNGRY EVERY DAY.

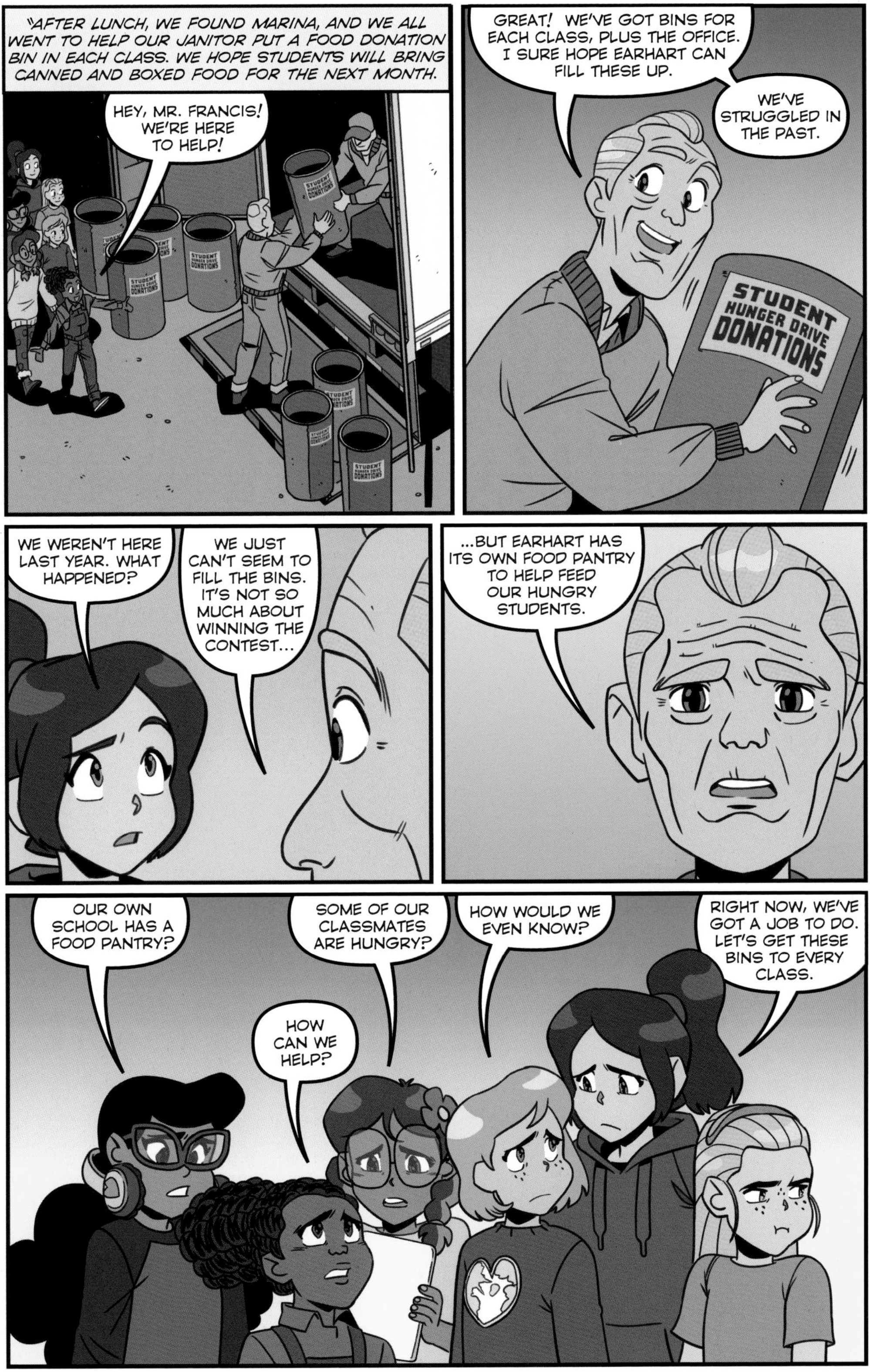

"AFTER LUNCH, WE FOUND MARINA, AND WE ALL WENT TO HELP OUR JANITOR PUT A FOOD DONATION BIN IN EACH CLASS. WE HOPE STUDENTS WILL BRING CANNED AND BOXED FOOD FOR THE NEXT MONTH.
HEY, MR. FRANCIS! WE'RE HERE TO HELP!
STUDENT HUNGER DRIVE DONATIONS
GREAT! WE'VE GOT BINS FOR EACH CLASS, PLUS THE OFFICE. I SURE HOPE EARHART CAN FILL THESE UP.
WE'VE STRUGGLED IN THE PAST.
STUDENT HUNGER DRIVE DONATIONS
WE WEREN'T HERE LAST YEAR. WHAT HAPPENED?
WE JUST CAN'T SEEM TO FILL THE BINS. IT'S NOT SO MUCH ABOUT WINNING THE CONTEST...
...BUT EARHART HAS ITS OWN FOOD PANTRY TO HELP FEED OUR HUNGRY STUDENTS.
OUR OWN SCHOOL HAS A FOOD PANTRY?
HOW CAN WE HELP?
SOME OF OUR CLASSMATES ARE HUNGRY?
HOW WOULD WE EVEN KNOW?
RIGHT NOW, WE'VE GOT A JOB TO DO. LET'S GET THESE BINS TO EVERY CLASS.

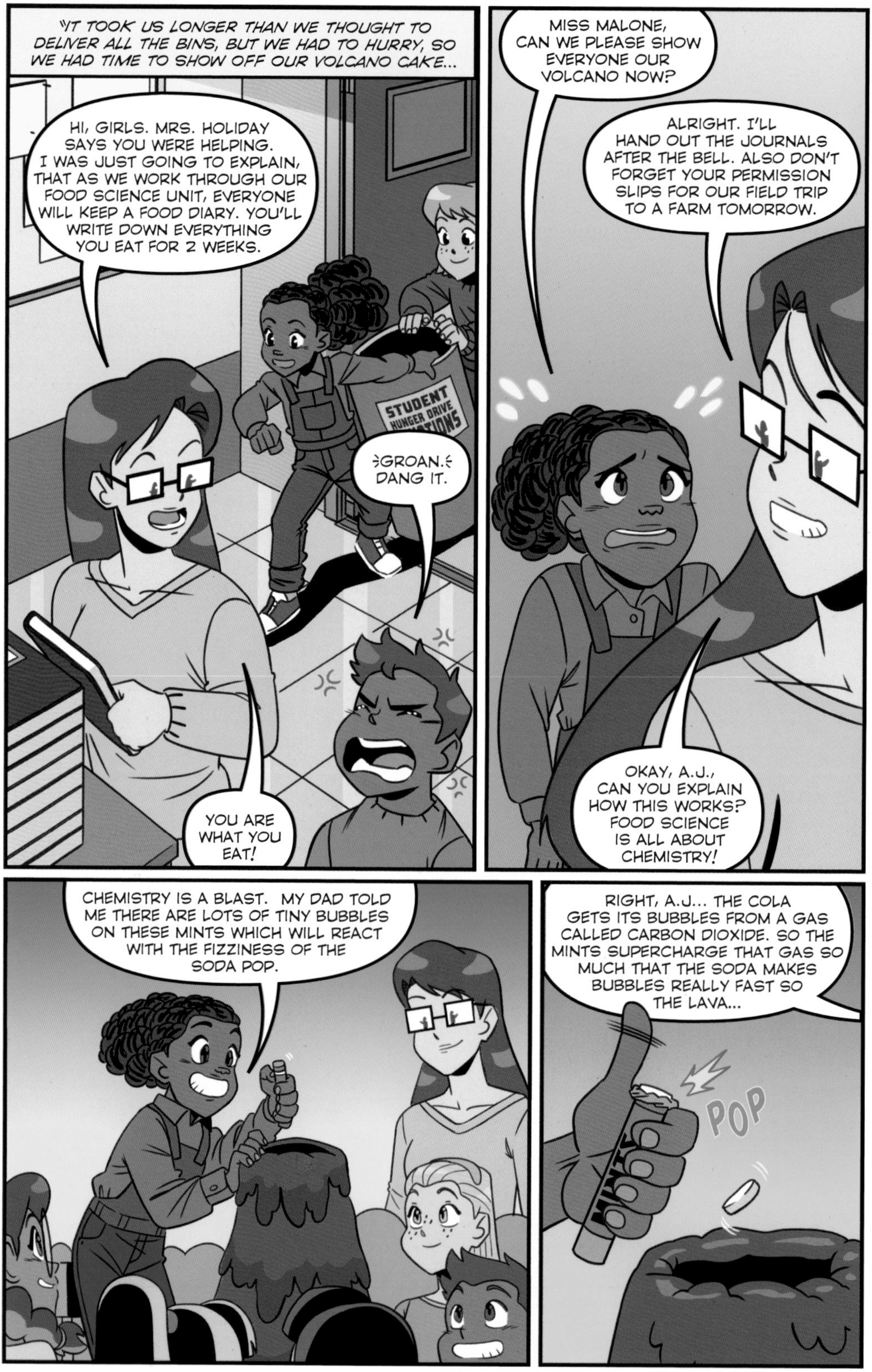
"IT TOOK US LONGER THAN WE THOUGHT TO DELIVER ALL THE BINS, BUT WE HAD TO HURRY, SO WE HAD TIME TO SHOW OFF OUR VOLCANO CAKE...
HI, GIRLS. MRS. HOLIDAY SAYS YOU WERE HELPING. I WAS JUST GOING TO EXPLAIN, THAT AS WE WORK THROUGH OUR FOOD SCIENCE UNIT, EVERYONE WILL KEEP A FOOD DIARY. YOU'LL WRITE DOWN EVERYTHING YOU EAT FOR 2 WEEKS.
STUDENT HUNGER DRIVE
GROAN. DANG IT.
YOU ARE WHAT YOU EAT!
MISS MALONE, CAN WE PLEASE SHOW EVERYONE OUR VOLCANO NOW?
ALRIGHT. I'LL HAND OUT THE JOURNALS AFTER THE BELL. ALSO DON'T FORGET YOUR PERMISSION SLIPS FOR OUR FIELD TRIP TO A FARM TOMORROW.
OKAY, A.J., CAN YOU EXPLAIN HOW THIS WORKS? FOOD SCIENCE IS ALL ABOUT CHEMISTRY!
CHEMISTRY IS A BLAST. MY DAD TOLD ME THERE ARE LOTS OF TINY BUBBLES ON THESE MINTS WHICH WILL REACT WITH THE FIZZINESS OF THE SODA POP.
RIGHT, A.J... THE COLA GETS ITS BUBBLES FROM A GAS CALLED CARBON DIOXIDE. SO THE MINTS SUPERCHARGE THAT GAS SO MUCH THAT THE SODA MAKES BUBBLES REALLY FAST SO THE LAVA...
POP
MINTS

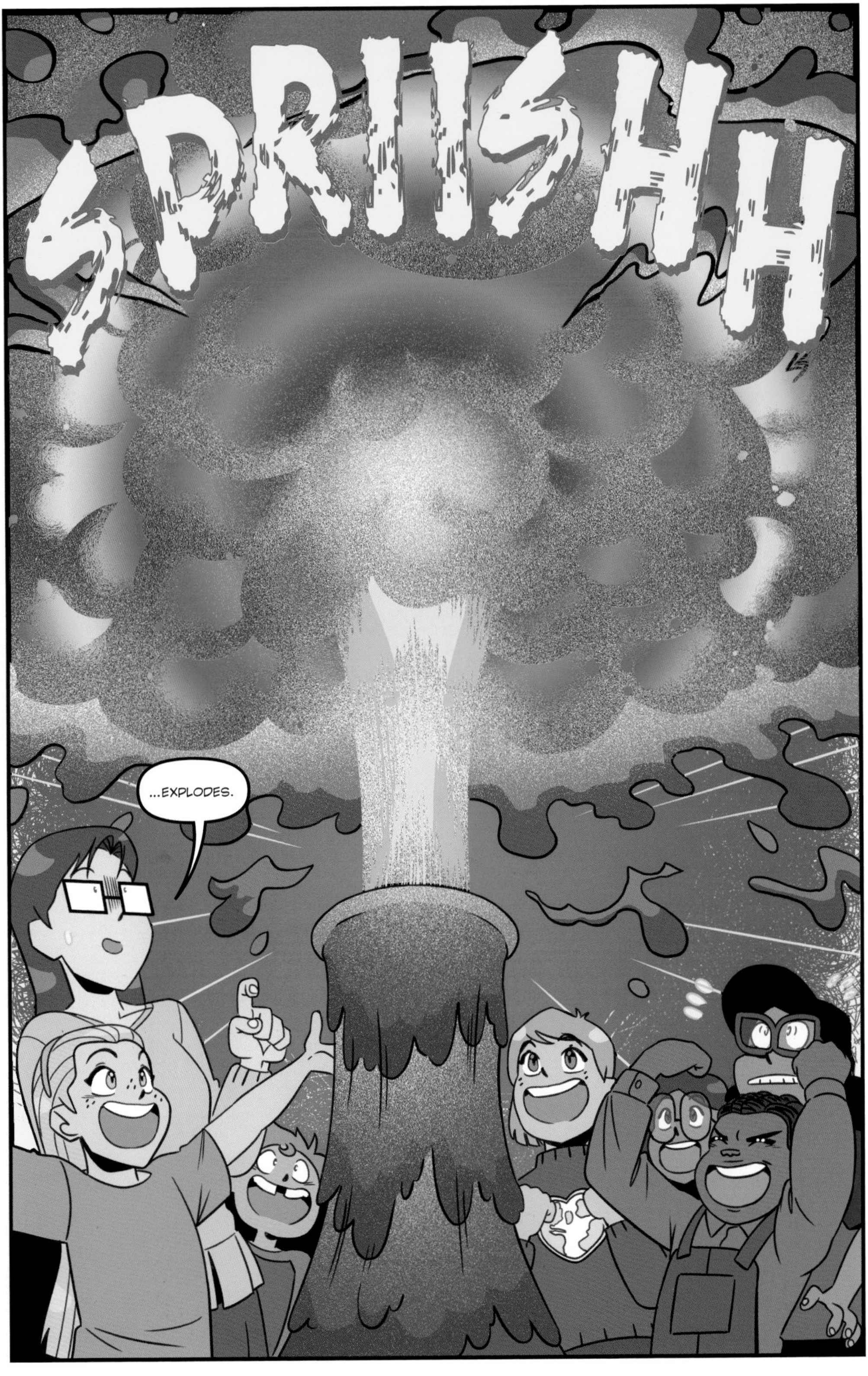
SPRIISHH
...EXPLODES.

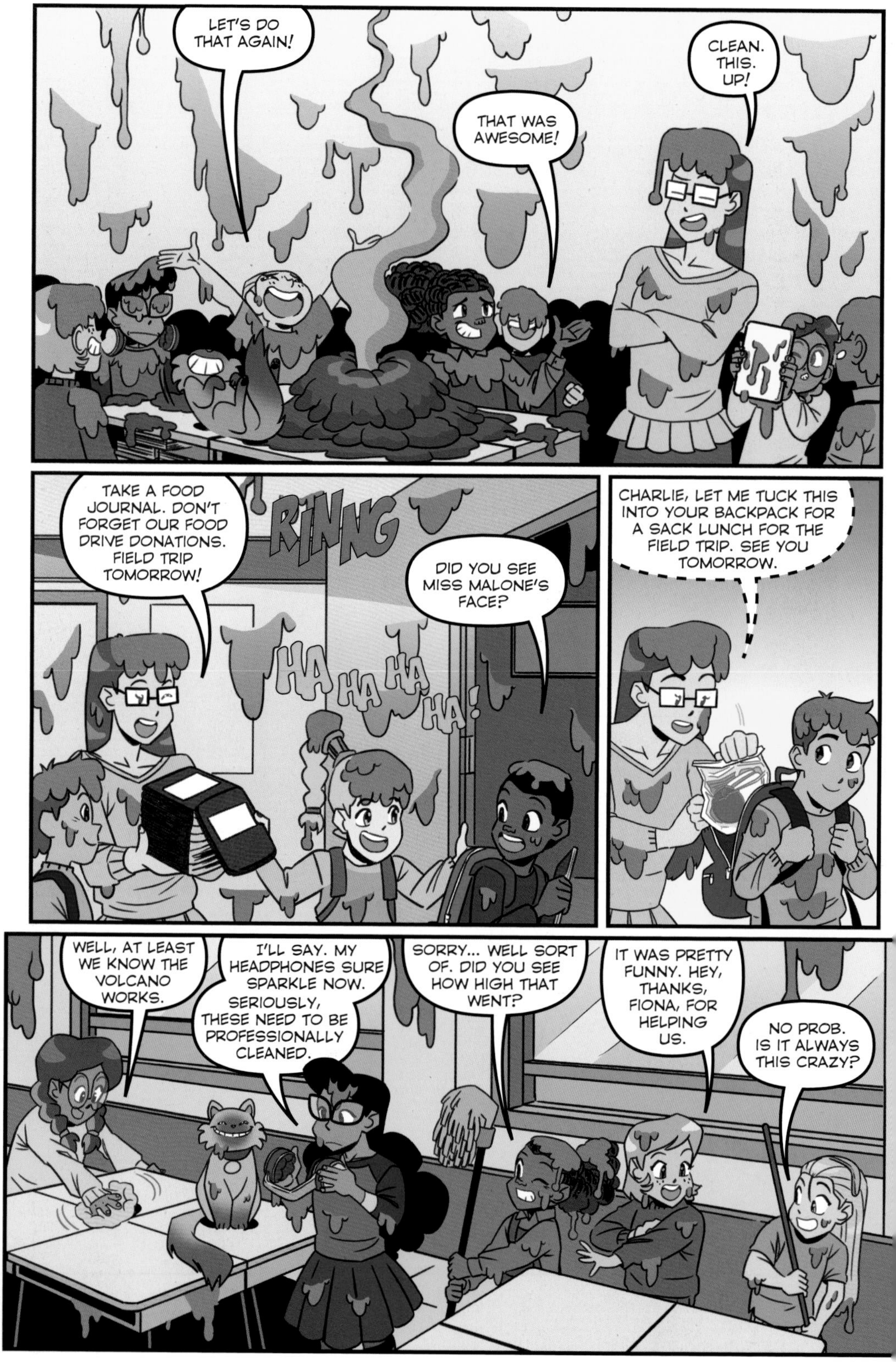
LET'S DO THAT AGAIN!
THAT WAS AWESOME!
CLEAN. THIS. UP!
TAKE A FOOD JOURNAL. DON'T FORGET OUR FOOD DRIVE DONATIONS. FIELD TRIP TOMORROW!
RING
HA HA HA HA!
DID YOU SEE MISS MALONE'S FACE?
CHARLIE, LET ME TUCK THIS INTO YOUR BACKPACK FOR A SACK LUNCH FOR THE FIELD TRIP. SEE YOU TOMORROW.
WELL, AT LEAST WE KNOW THE VOLCANO WORKS.
I'LL SAY. MY HEADPHONES SURE SPARKLE NOW.
SERIOUSLY, THESE NEED TO BE PROFESSIONALLY CLEANED.
SORRY... WELL SORT OF. DID YOU SEE HOW HIGH THAT WENT?
IT WAS PRETTY FUNNY. HEY, THANKS, FIONA, FOR HELPING US.
NO PROB. IS IT ALWAYS THIS CRAZY?

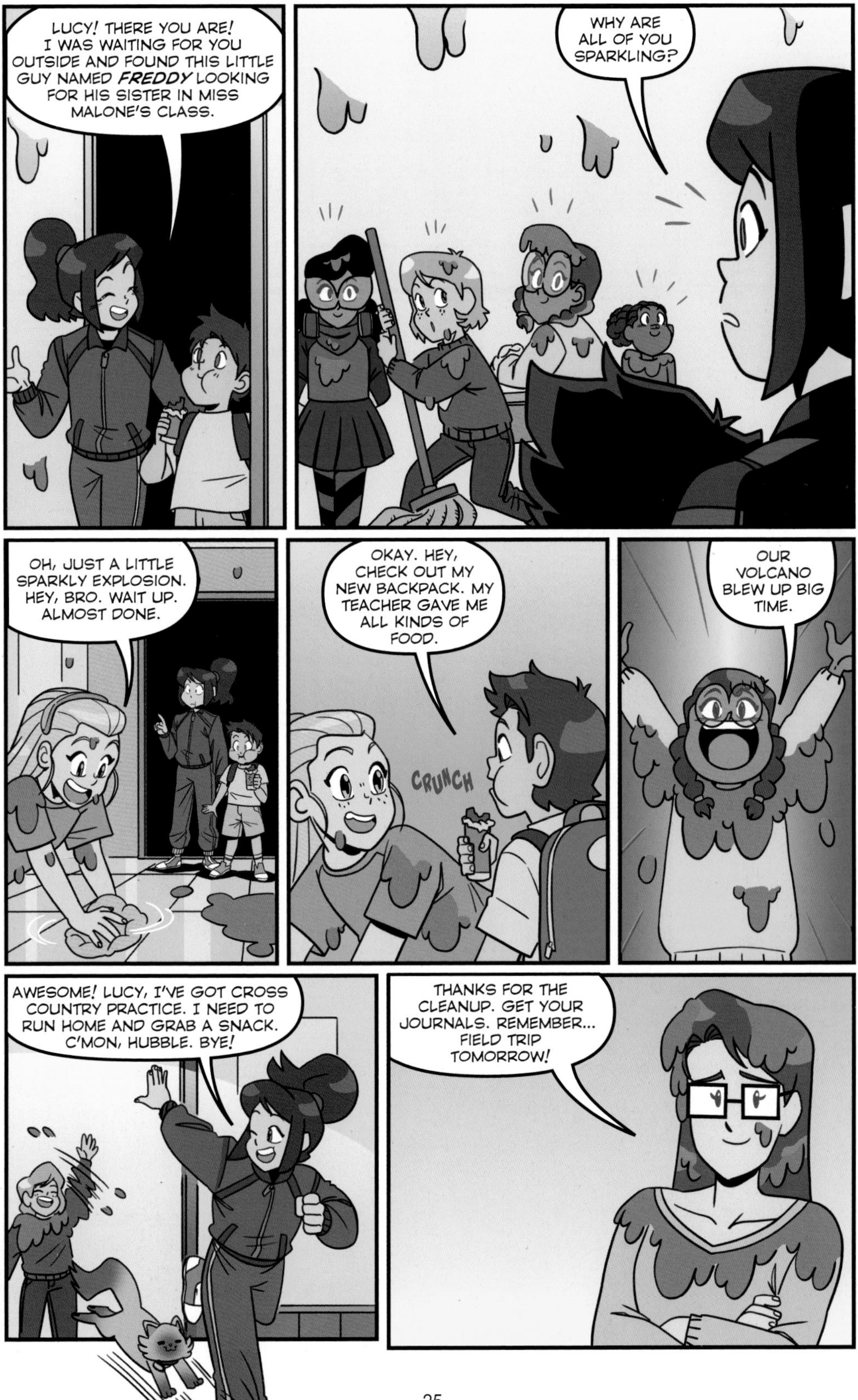
LUCY! THERE YOU ARE! I WAS WAITING FOR YOU OUTSIDE AND FOUND THIS LITTLE GUY NAMED *FREDDY* LOOKING FOR HIS SISTER IN MISS MALONE'S CLASS.
WHY ARE ALL OF YOU SPARKLING?
OH, JUST A LITTLE SPARKLY EXPLOSION. HEY, BRO. WAIT UP. ALMOST DONE.
OKAY. HEY, CHECK OUT MY NEW BACKPACK. MY TEACHER GAVE ME ALL KINDS OF FOOD.
CRUNCH
OUR VOLCANO BLEW UP BIG TIME.
AWESOME! LUCY, I'VE GOT CROSS COUNTRY PRACTICE. I NEED TO RUN HOME AND GRAB A SNACK. C'MON, HUBBLE. BYE!
THANKS FOR THE CLEANUP. GET YOUR JOURNALS. REMEMBER... FIELD TRIP TOMORROW!

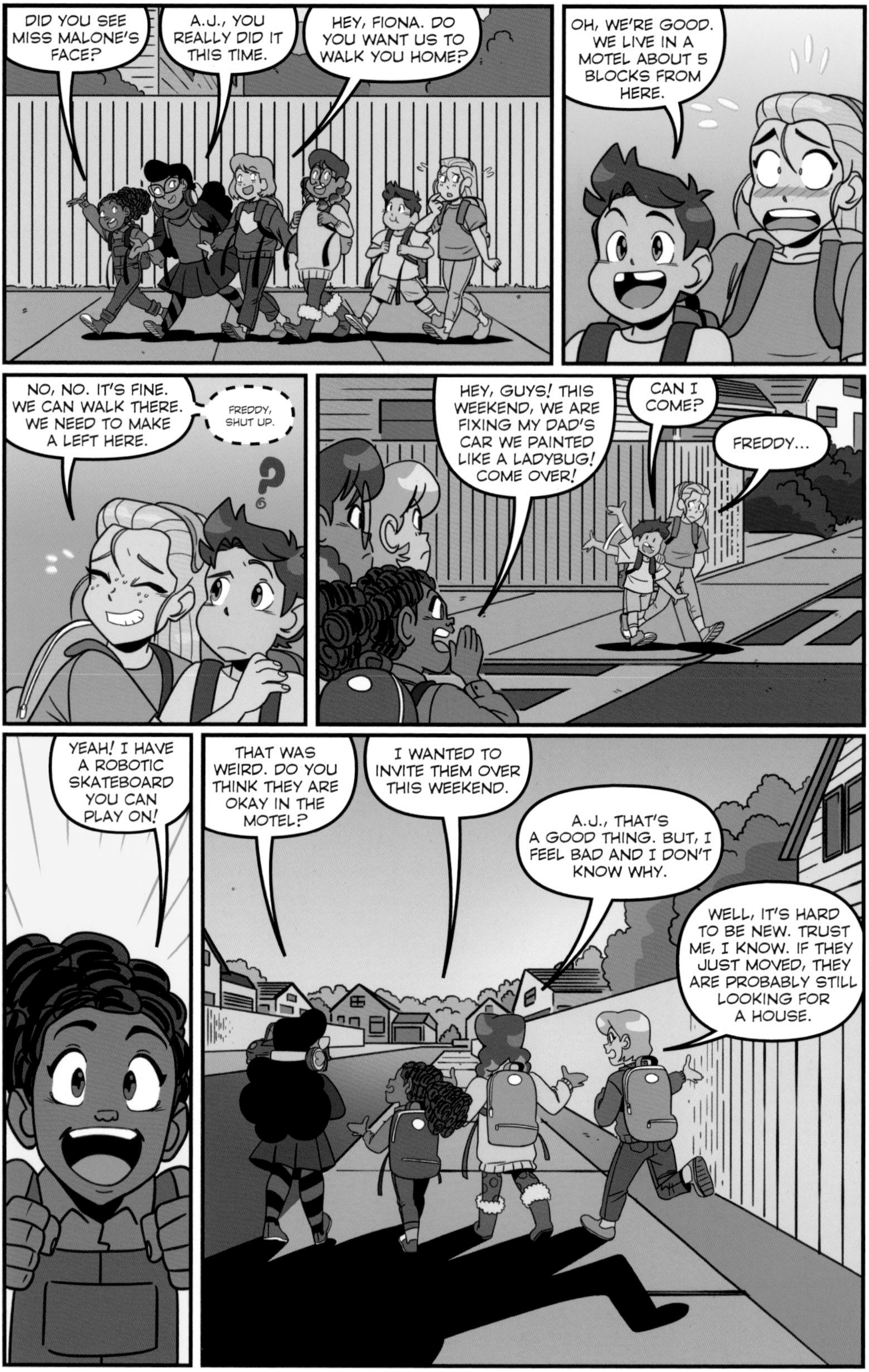
DID YOU SEE MISS MALONE'S FACE?
A.J., YOU REALLY DID IT THIS TIME.
HEY, FIONA. DO YOU WANT US TO WALK YOU HOME?
OH, WE'RE GOOD. WE LIVE IN A MOTEL ABOUT 5 BLOCKS FROM HERE.
NO, NO. IT'S FINE. WE CAN WALK THERE. WE NEED TO MAKE A LEFT HERE.
FREDDY, SHUT UP.
HEY, GUYS! THIS WEEKEND, WE ARE FIXING MY DAD'S CAR WE PAINTED LIKE A LADYBUG! COME OVER!
CAN I COME?
FREDDY...
YEAH! I HAVE A ROBOTIC SKATEBOARD YOU CAN PLAY ON!
THAT WAS WEIRD. DO YOU THINK THEY ARE OKAY IN THE MOTEL?
I WANTED TO INVITE THEM OVER THIS WEEKEND.
A.J., THAT'S A GOOD THING. BUT, I FEEL BAD AND I DON'T KNOW WHY.
WELL, IT'S HARD TO BE NEW. TRUST ME, I KNOW. IF THEY JUST MOVED, THEY ARE PROBABLY STILL LOOKING FOR A HOUSE.

CHAPTER FOUR: A FARM GIRL NAMED FIONA

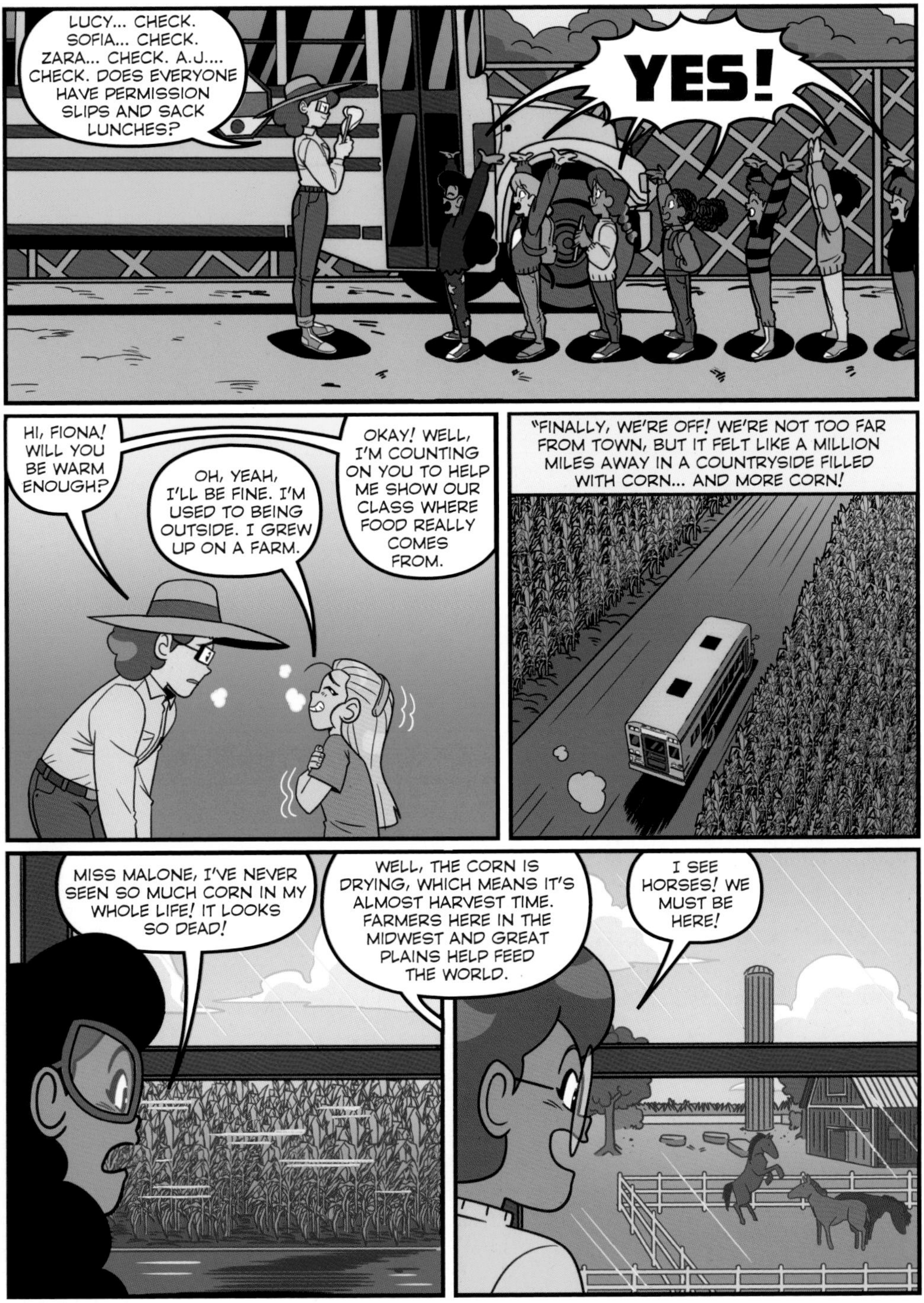
LUCY... CHECK. SOFIA... CHECK. ZARA... CHECK. A.J.... CHECK. DOES EVERYONE HAVE PERMISSION SLIPS AND SACK LUNCHES?
YES!
HI, FIONA! WILL YOU BE WARM ENOUGH?
OH, YEAH, I'LL BE FINE. I'M USED TO BEING OUTSIDE. I GREW UP ON A FARM.
OKAY! WELL, I'M COUNTING ON YOU TO HELP ME SHOW OUR CLASS WHERE FOOD REALLY COMES FROM.
"FINALLY, WE'RE OFF! WE'RE NOT TOO FAR FROM TOWN, BUT IT FELT LIKE A MILLION MILES AWAY IN A COUNTRYSIDE FILLED WITH CORN... AND MORE CORN!
MISS MALONE, I'VE NEVER SEEN SO MUCH CORN IN MY WHOLE LIFE! IT LOOKS SO DEAD!
WELL, THE CORN IS DRYING, WHICH MEANS IT'S ALMOST HARVEST TIME. FARMERS HERE IN THE MIDWEST AND GREAT PLAINS HELP FEED THE WORLD.
I SEE HORSES! WE MUST BE HERE!

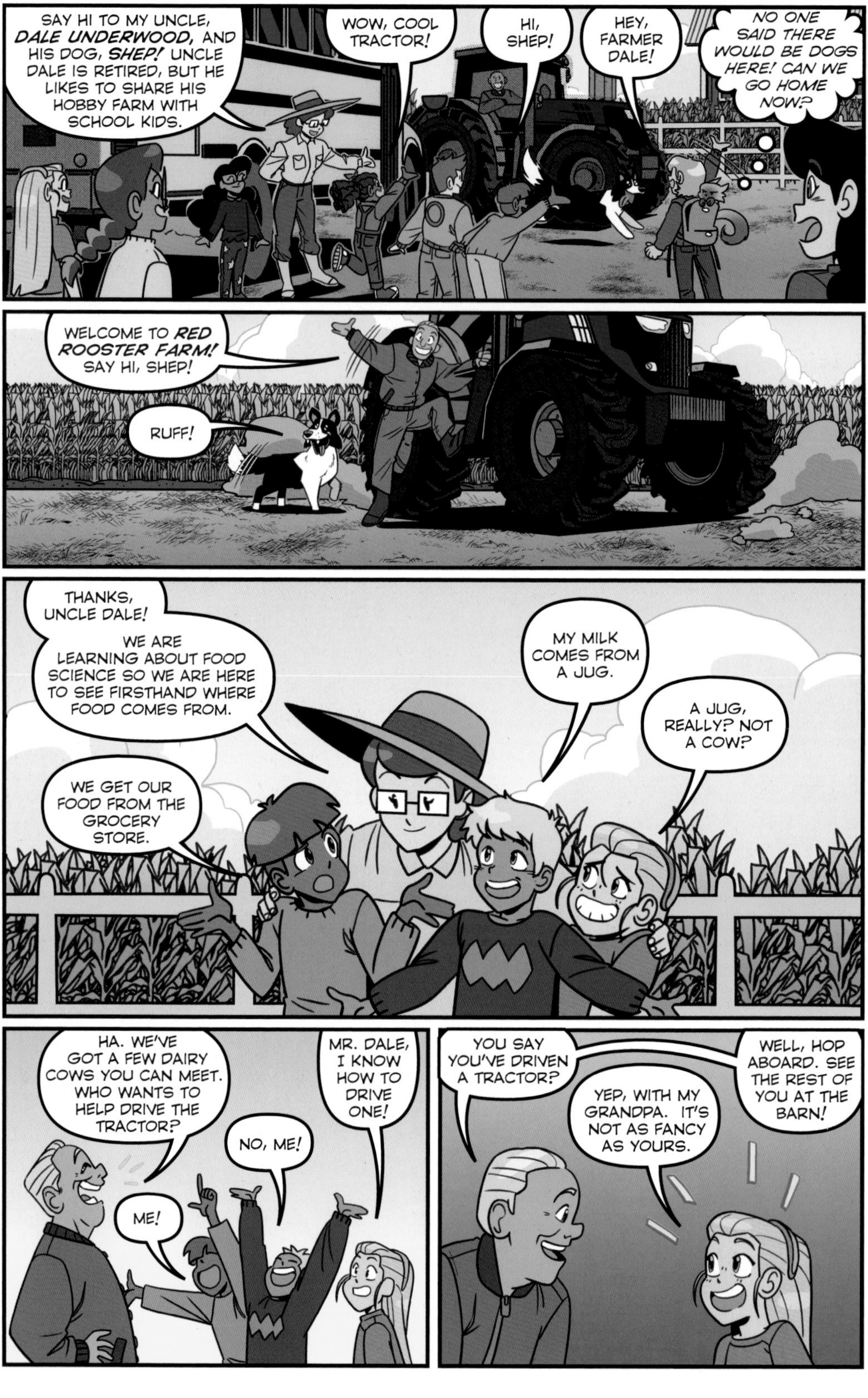

SAY HI TO MY UNCLE, DALE UNDERWOOD, AND HIS DOG, SHEP! UNCLE DALE IS RETIRED, BUT HE LIKES TO SHARE HIS HOBBY FARM WITH SCHOOL KIDS.
WOW, COOL TRACTOR!
HI, SHEP!
HEY, FARMER DALE!
NO ONE SAID THERE WOULD BE DOGS HERE! CAN WE GO HOME NOW?
WELCOME TO RED ROOSTER FARM! SAY HI, SHEP!
RUFF!
THANKS, UNCLE DALE!
WE ARE LEARNING ABOUT FOOD SCIENCE SO WE ARE HERE TO SEE FIRSTHAND WHERE FOOD COMES FROM.
MY MILK COMES FROM A JUG.
A JUG, REALLY? NOT A COW?
WE GET OUR FOOD FROM THE GROCERY STORE.
HA. WE'VE GOT A FEW DAIRY COWS YOU CAN MEET. WHO WANTS TO HELP DRIVE THE TRACTOR?
MR. DALE, I KNOW HOW TO DRIVE ONE!
NO, ME!
ME!
YOU SAY YOU'VE DRIVEN A TRACTOR?
WELL, HOP ABOARD. SEE THE REST OF YOU AT THE BARN!
YEP, WITH MY GRANDPA. IT'S NOT AS FANCY AS YOURS.

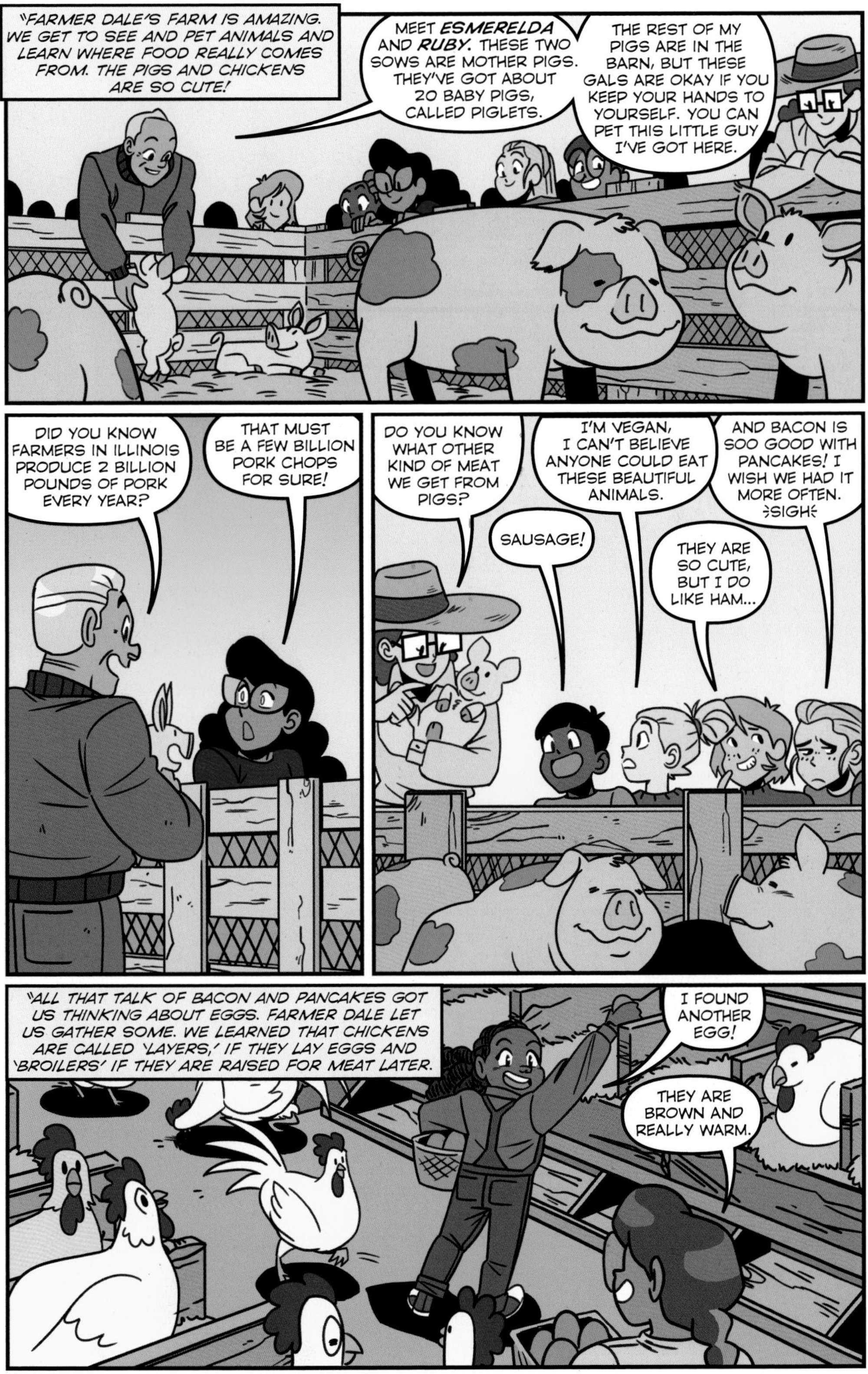

"FARMER DALE'S FARM IS AMAZING. WE GET TO SEE AND PET ANIMALS AND LEARN WHERE FOOD REALLY COMES FROM. THE PIGS AND CHICKENS ARE SO CUTE!
MEET ESMERELDA AND RUBY. THESE TWO SOWS ARE MOTHER PIGS. THEY'VE GOT ABOUT 20 BABY PIGS, CALLED PIGLETS.
THE REST OF MY PIGS ARE IN THE BARN, BUT THESE GALS ARE OKAY IF YOU KEEP YOUR HANDS TO YOURSELF. YOU CAN PET THIS LITTLE GUY I'VE GOT HERE.
DID YOU KNOW FARMERS IN ILLINOIS PRODUCE 2 BILLION POUNDS OF PORK EVERY YEAR?
THAT MUST BE A FEW BILLION PORK CHOPS FOR SURE!
DO YOU KNOW WHAT OTHER KIND OF MEAT WE GET FROM PIGS?
SAUSAGE!
I'M VEGAN, I CAN'T BELIEVE ANYONE COULD EAT THESE BEAUTIFUL ANIMALS.
THEY ARE SO CUTE, BUT I DO LIKE HAM...
AND BACON IS SOO GOOD WITH PANCAKES! I WISH WE HAD IT MORE OFTEN. ≯SIGH≮
"ALL THAT TALK OF BACON AND PANCAKES GOT US THINKING ABOUT EGGS. FARMER DALE LET US GATHER SOME. WE LEARNED THAT CHICKENS ARE CALLED 'LAYERS,' IF THEY LAY EGGS AND 'BROILERS' IF THEY ARE RAISED FOR MEAT LATER.
I FOUND ANOTHER EGG!
THEY ARE BROWN AND REALLY WARM.

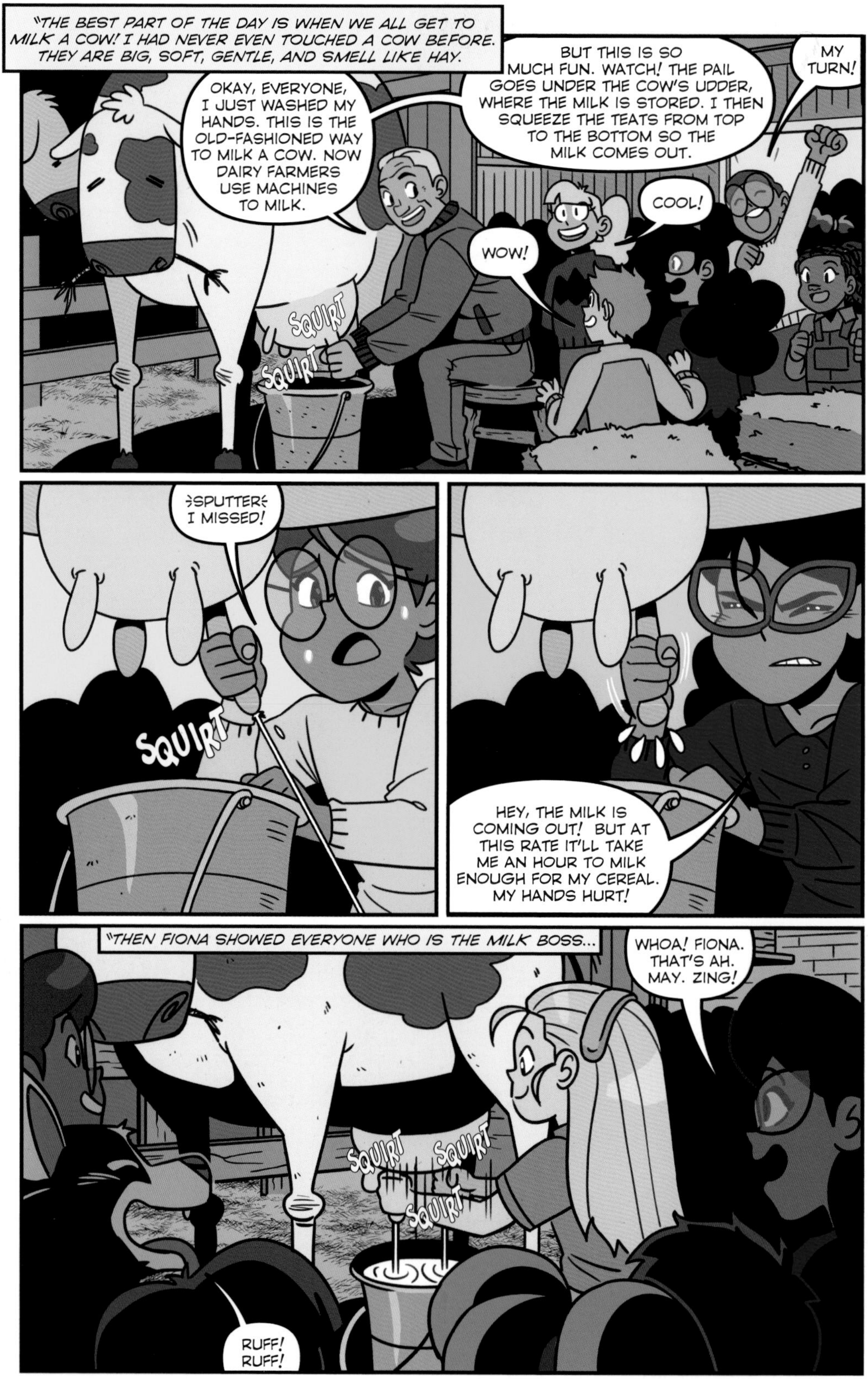
"THE BEST PART OF THE DAY IS WHEN WE ALL GET TO MILK A COW! I HAD NEVER EVEN TOUCHED A COW BEFORE. THEY ARE BIG, SOFT, GENTLE, AND SMELL LIKE HAY.
OKAY, EVERYONE, I JUST WASHED MY HANDS. THIS IS THE OLD-FASHIONED WAY TO MILK A COW. NOW DAIRY FARMERS USE MACHINES TO MILK.
BUT THIS IS SO MUCH FUN. WATCH! THE PAIL GOES UNDER THE COW'S UDDER, WHERE THE MILK IS STORED. I THEN SQUEEZE THE TEATS FROM TOP TO THE BOTTOM SO THE MILK COMES OUT.
MY TURN!
COOL!
WOW!
SQUIRT
SQUIRT
SPUTTER I MISSED!
SQUIRT
HEY, THE MILK IS COMING OUT! BUT AT THIS RATE IT'LL TAKE ME AN HOUR TO MILK ENOUGH FOR MY CEREAL. MY HANDS HURT!
"THEN FIONA SHOWED EVERYONE WHO IS THE MILK BOSS...
WHOA! FIONA. THAT'S AH. MAY. ZING!
SQUIRT
SQUIRT
SQUIRT
RUFF! RUFF!

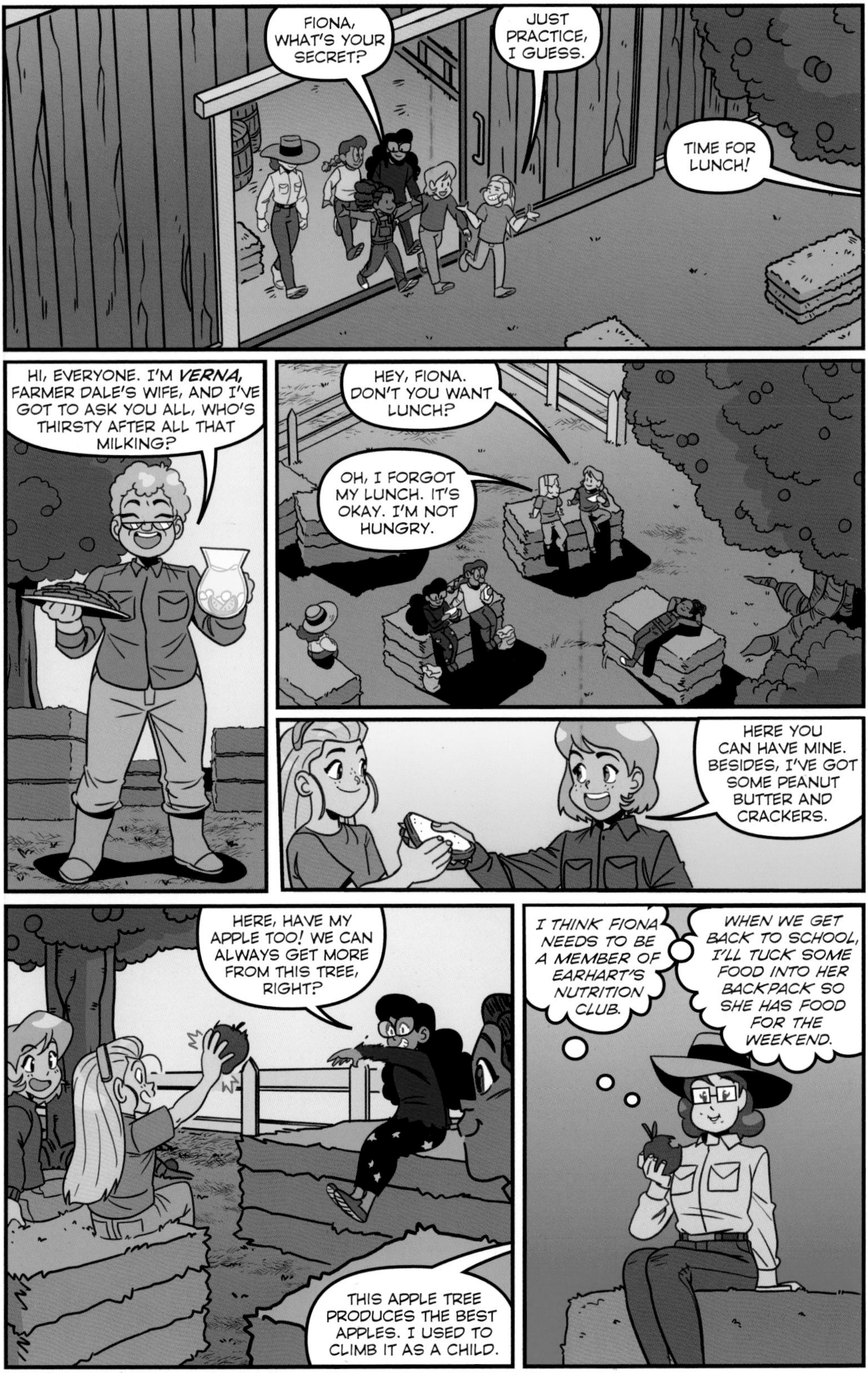
FIONA, WHAT'S YOUR SECRET?
JUST PRACTICE, I GUESS.
TIME FOR LUNCH!
HI, EVERYONE. I'M *VERNA,* FARMER DALE'S WIFE, AND I'VE GOT TO ASK YOU ALL, WHO'S THIRSTY AFTER ALL THAT MILKING?
HEY, FIONA. DON'T YOU WANT LUNCH?
OH, I FORGOT MY LUNCH. IT'S OKAY. I'M NOT HUNGRY.
HERE YOU CAN HAVE MINE. BESIDES, I'VE GOT SOME PEANUT BUTTER AND CRACKERS.
HERE, HAVE MY APPLE TOO! WE CAN ALWAYS GET MORE FROM THIS TREE, RIGHT?
THIS APPLE TREE PRODUCES THE BEST APPLES. I USED TO CLIMB IT AS A CHILD.
I THINK FIONA NEEDS TO BE A MEMBER OF EARHART'S NUTRITION CLUB.
WHEN WE GET BACK TO SCHOOL, I'LL TUCK SOME FOOD INTO HER BACKPACK SO SHE HAS FOOD FOR THE WEEKEND.

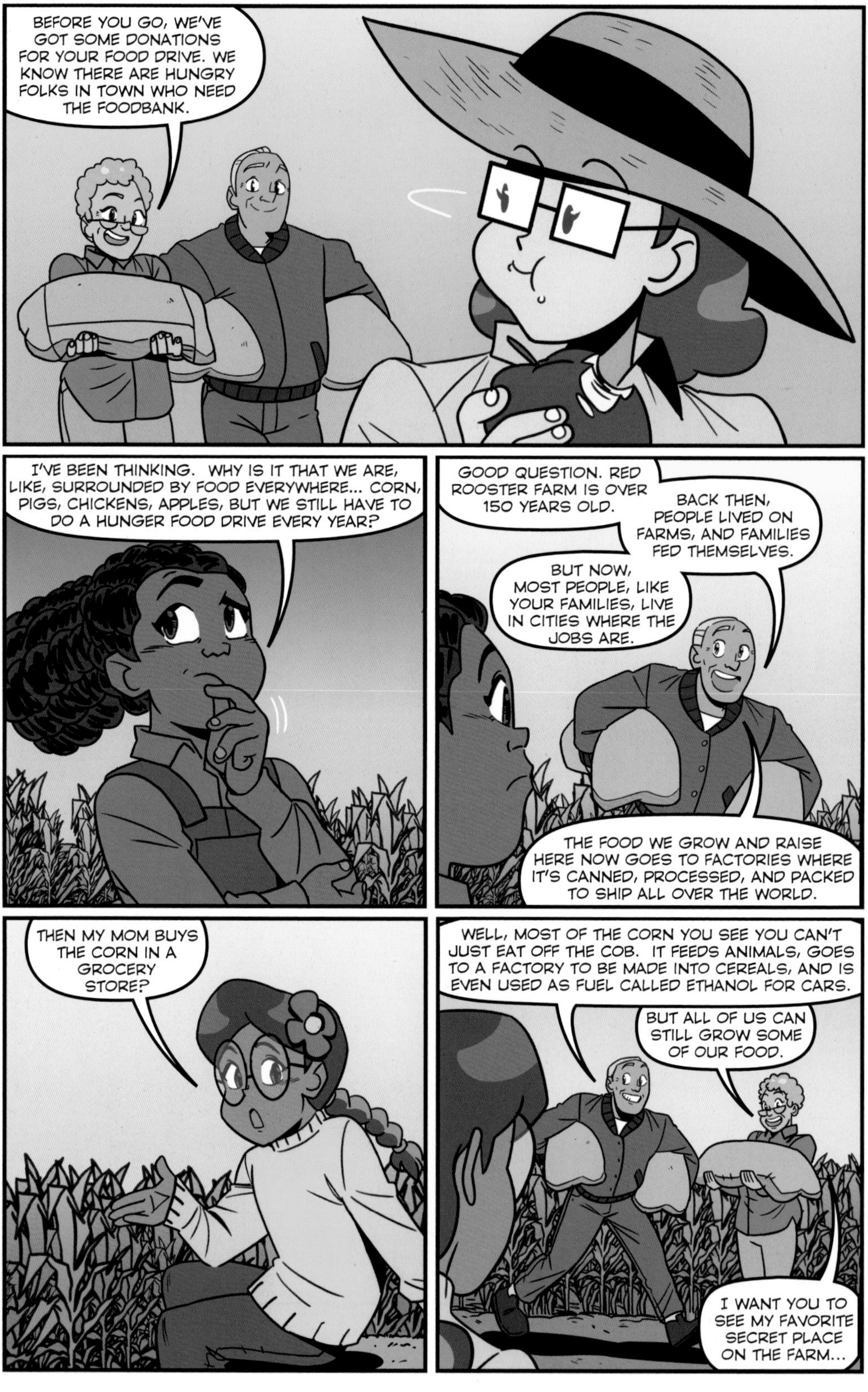
BEFORE YOU GO, WE'VE GOT SOME DONATIONS FOR YOUR FOOD DRIVE. WE KNOW THERE ARE HUNGRY FOLKS IN TOWN WHO NEED THE FOODBANK.
I'VE BEEN THINKING. WHY IS IT THAT WE ARE, LIKE, SURROUNDED BY FOOD EVERYWHERE... CORN, PIGS, CHICKENS, APPLES, BUT WE STILL HAVE TO DO A HUNGER FOOD DRIVE EVERY YEAR?
GOOD QUESTION. RED ROOSTER FARM IS OVER 150 YEARS OLD.
BACK THEN, PEOPLE LIVED ON FARMS, AND FAMILIES FED THEMSELVES.
BUT NOW, MOST PEOPLE, LIKE YOUR FAMILIES, LIVE IN CITIES WHERE THE JOBS ARE.
THE FOOD WE GROW AND RAISE HERE NOW GOES TO FACTORIES WHERE IT'S CANNED, PROCESSED, AND PACKED TO SHIP ALL OVER THE WORLD.
THEN MY MOM BUYS THE CORN IN A GROCERY STORE?
WELL, MOST OF THE CORN YOU SEE YOU CAN'T JUST EAT OFF THE COB. IT FEEDS ANIMALS, GOES TO A FACTORY TO BE MADE INTO CEREALS, AND IS EVEN USED AS FUEL CALLED ETHANOL FOR CARS.
BUT ALL OF US CAN STILL GROW SOME OF OUR FOOD.
I WANT YOU TO SEE MY FAVORITE SECRET PLACE ON THE FARM...

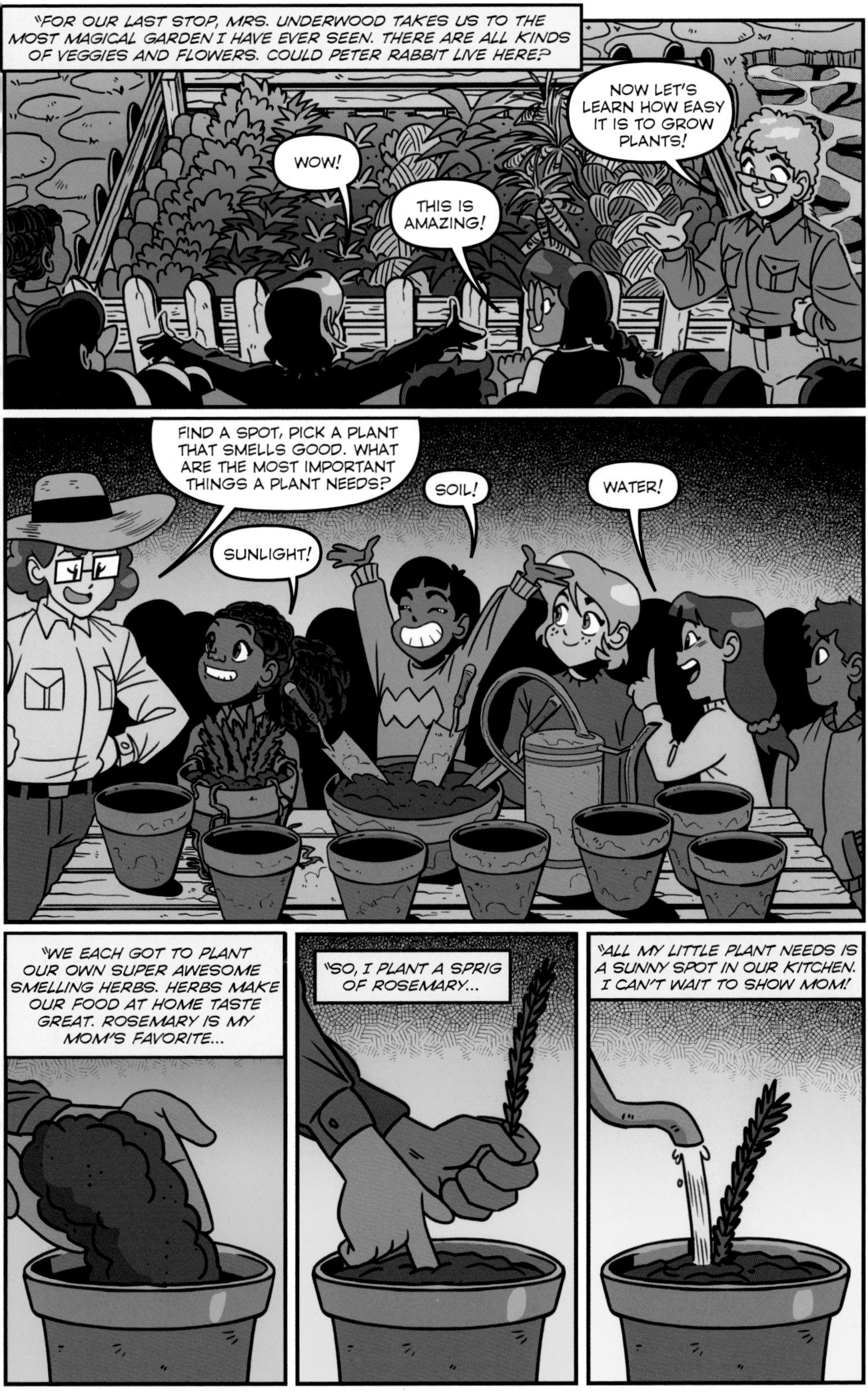
"FOR OUR LAST STOP, MRS. UNDERWOOD TAKES US TO THE MOST MAGICAL GARDEN I HAVE EVER SEEN. THERE ARE ALL KINDS OF VEGGIES AND FLOWERS. COULD PETER RABBIT LIVE HERE?
WOW!
THIS IS AMAZING!
NOW LET'S LEARN HOW EASY IT IS TO GROW PLANTS!
FIND A SPOT, PICK A PLANT THAT SMELLS GOOD. WHAT ARE THE MOST IMPORTANT THINGS A PLANT NEEDS?
SUNLIGHT!
SOIL!
WATER!
"WE EACH GOT TO PLANT OUR OWN SUPER AWESOME SMELLING HERBS. HERBS MAKE OUR FOOD AT HOME TASTE GREAT. ROSEMARY IS MY MOM'S FAVORITE...
"SO, I PLANT A SPRIG OF ROSEMARY...
"ALL MY LITTLE PLANT NEEDS IS A SUNNY SPOT IN OUR KITCHEN. I CAN'T WAIT TO SHOW MOM!

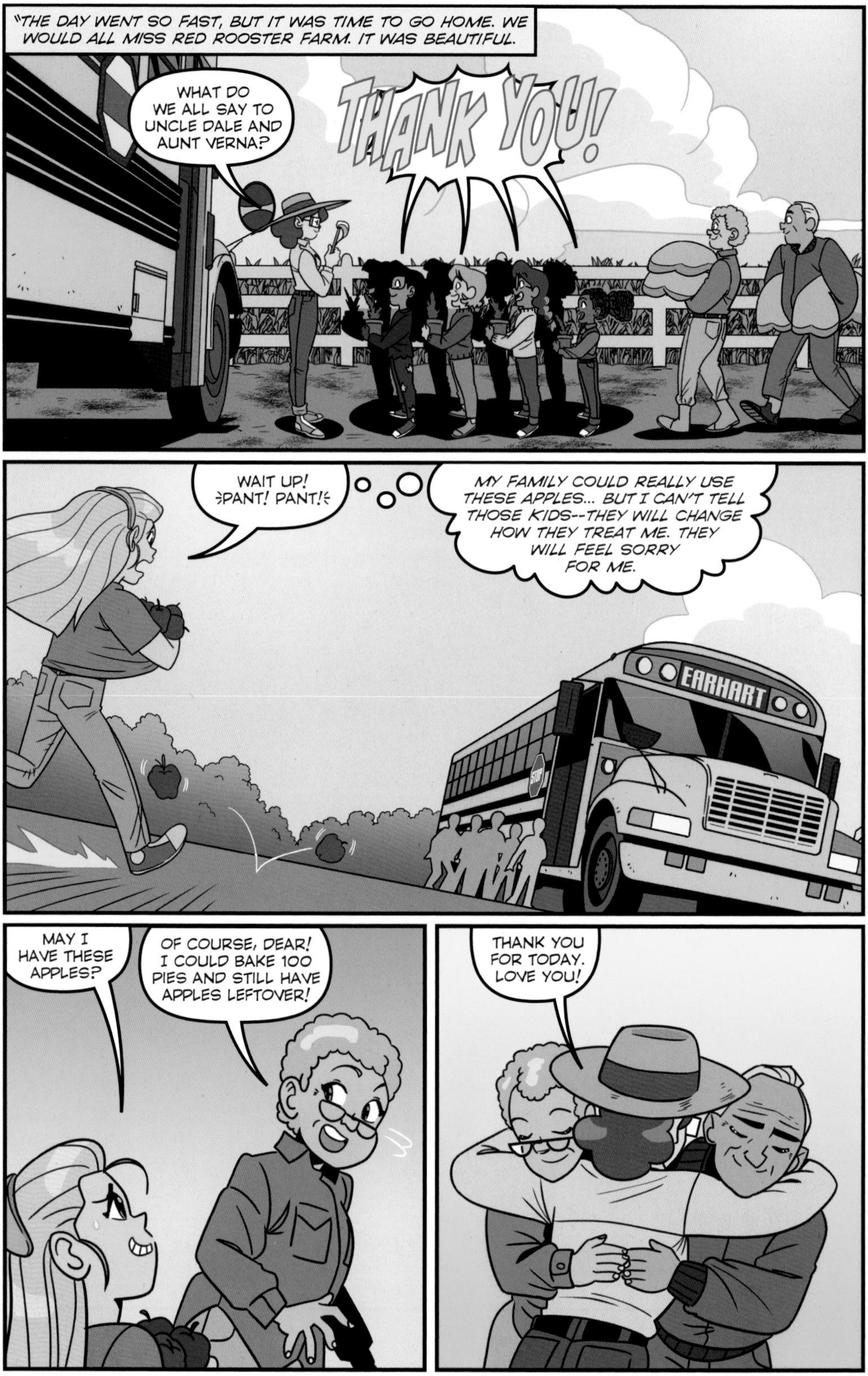
"THE DAY WENT SO FAST, BUT IT WAS TIME TO GO HOME. WE WOULD ALL MISS RED ROOSTER FARM. IT WAS BEAUTIFUL.
WHAT DO WE ALL SAY TO UNCLE DALE AND AUNT VERNA?
THANK YOU!
WAIT UP! PANT! PANT!
MY FAMILY COULD REALLY USE THESE APPLES... BUT I CAN'T TELL THOSE KIDS--THEY WILL CHANGE HOW THEY TREAT ME. THEY WILL FEEL SORRY FOR ME.
EARHART
STOP
MAY I HAVE THESE APPLES?
OF COURSE, DEAR! I COULD BAKE 100 PIES AND STILL HAVE APPLES LEFTOVER!
THANK YOU FOR TODAY. LOVE YOU!

CHAPTER FIVE: STRAWBERRY LADYBUGS AND PINEAPPLE FLOWERS

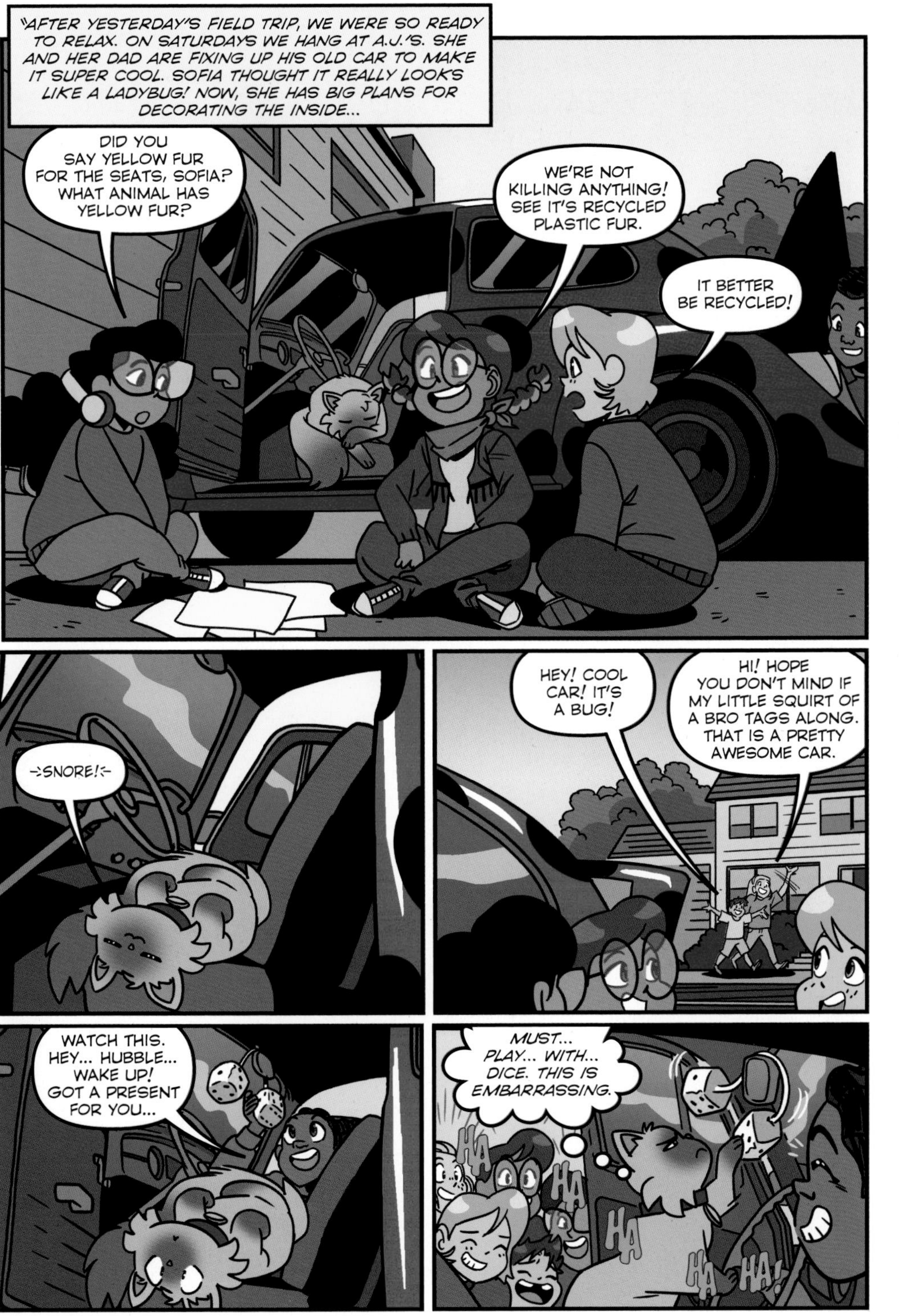
"AFTER YESTERDAY'S FIELD TRIP, WE WERE SO READY TO RELAX. ON SATURDAYS WE HANG AT A.J.'S. SHE AND HER DAD ARE FIXING UP HIS OLD CAR TO MAKE IT SUPER COOL. SOFIA THOUGHT IT REALLY LOOKS LIKE A LADYBUG! NOW, SHE HAS BIG PLANS FOR DECORATING THE INSIDE...
DID YOU SAY YELLOW FUR FOR THE SEATS, SOFIA? WHAT ANIMAL HAS YELLOW FUR?
WE'RE NOT KILLING ANYTHING! SEE IT'S RECYCLED PLASTIC FUR.
IT BETTER BE RECYCLED!
-SNORE!-
HEY! COOL CAR! IT'S A BUG!
HI! HOPE YOU DON'T MIND IF MY LITTLE SQUIRT OF A BRO TAGS ALONG. THAT IS A PRETTY AWESOME CAR.
WATCH THIS. HEY... HUBBLE... WAKE UP! GOT A PRESENT FOR YOU...
MUST... PLAY... WITH... DICE. THIS IS EMBARRASSING.
HA
HA
HA
HA
HA!

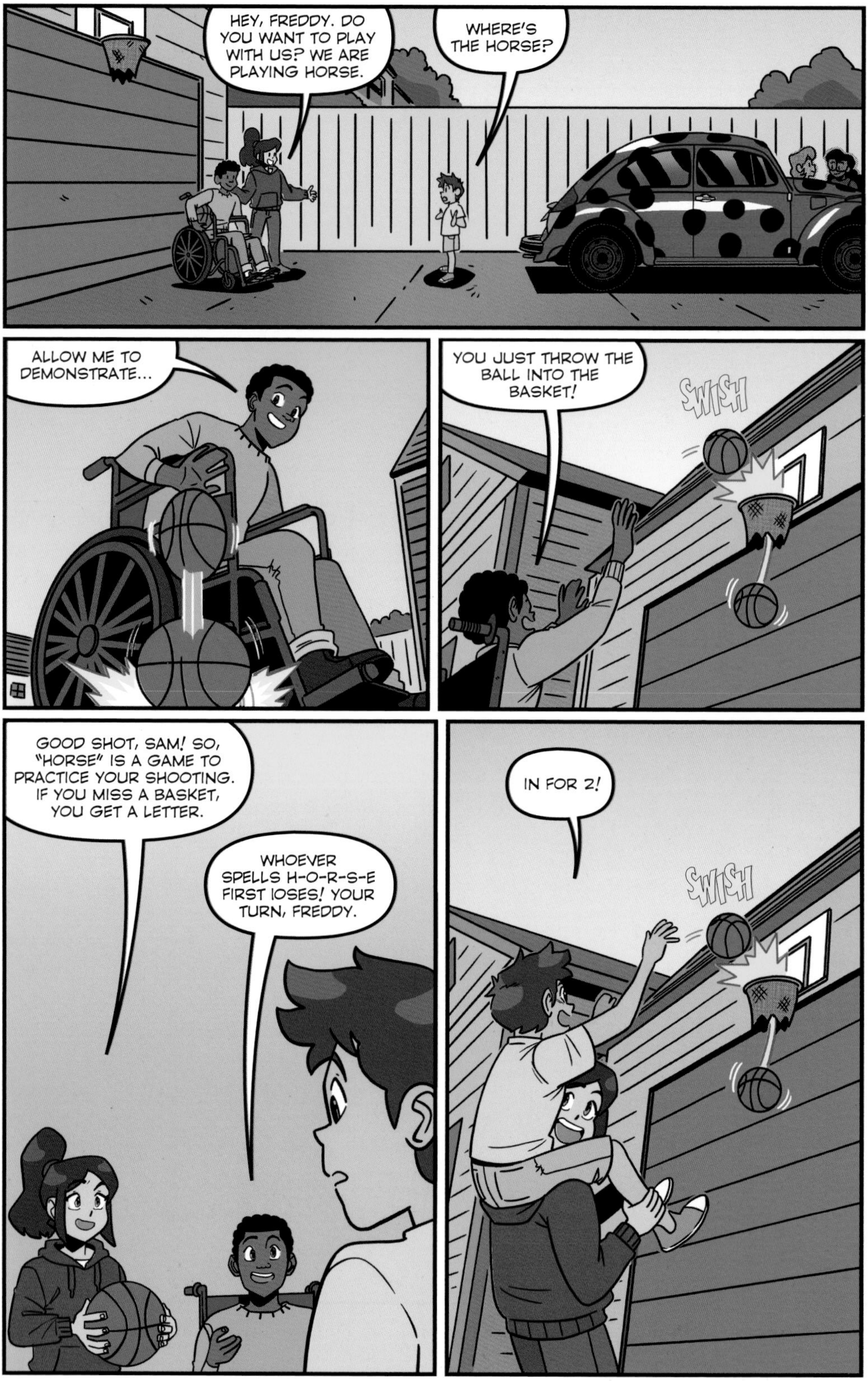

HEY, FREDDY. DO YOU WANT TO PLAY WITH US? WE ARE PLAYING HORSE.
WHERE'S THE HORSE?
ALLOW ME TO DEMONSTRATE...
YOU JUST THROW THE BALL INTO THE BASKET!
SWISH
GOOD SHOT, SAM! SO, "HORSE" IS A GAME TO PRACTICE YOUR SHOOTING. IF YOU MISS A BASKET, YOU GET A LETTER.
WHOEVER SPELLS H-O-R-S-E FIRST loSES! YOUR TURN, FREDDY.
IN FOR 2!
SWISH

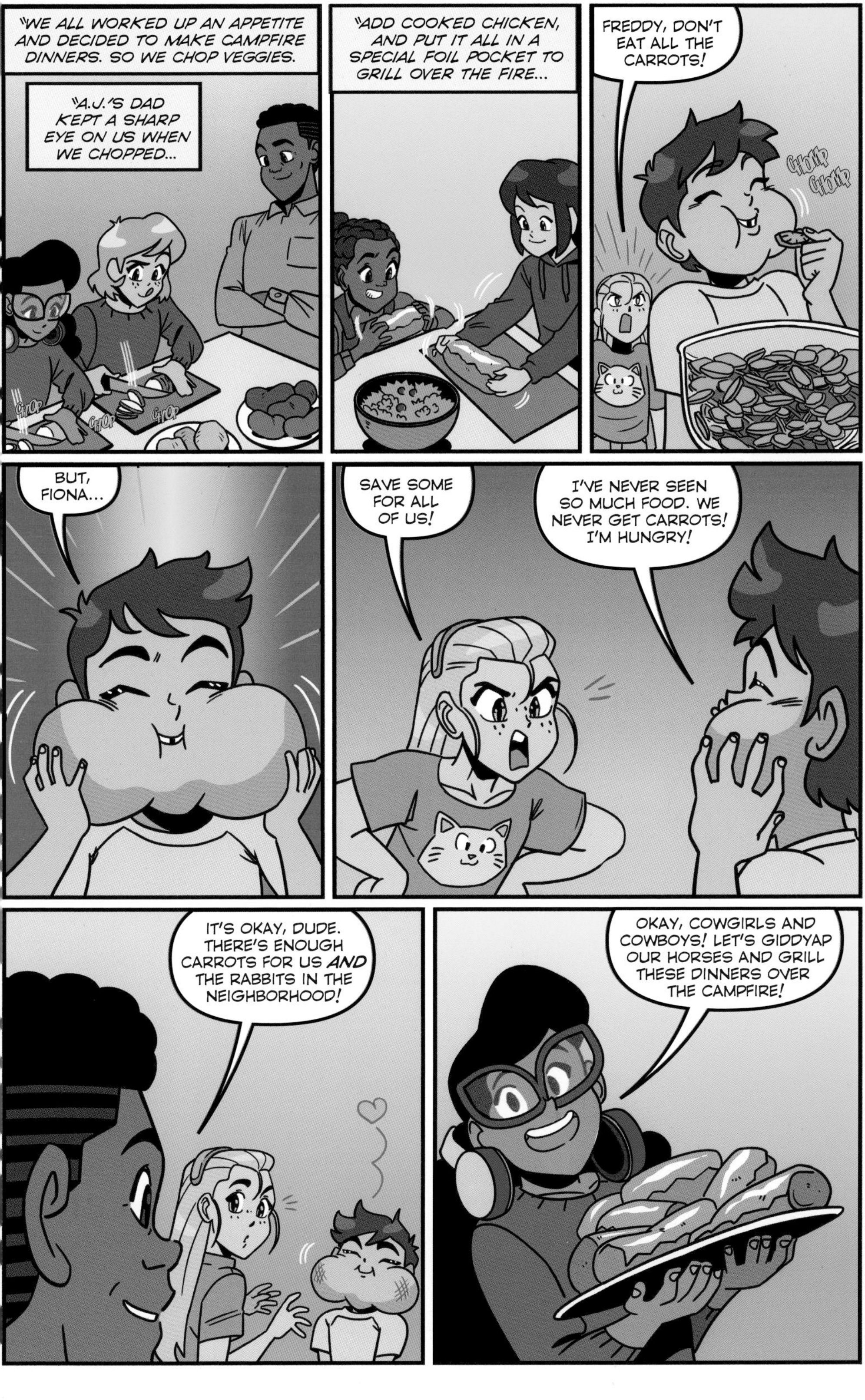
"WE ALL WORKED UP AN APPETITE AND DECIDED TO MAKE CAMPFIRE DINNERS. SO WE CHOP VEGGIES.
"A.J.'S DAD KEPT A SHARP EYE ON US WHEN WE CHOPPED...
CHOP
CHOP
CHOP
"ADD COOKED CHICKEN, AND PUT IT ALL IN A SPECIAL FOIL POCKET TO GRILL OVER THE FIRE...
FREDDY, DON'T EAT ALL THE CARROTS!
CHOMP
CHOMP
BUT, FIONA...
SAVE SOME FOR ALL OF US!
I'VE NEVER SEEN SO MUCH FOOD. WE NEVER GET CARROTS! I'M HUNGRY!
IT'S OKAY, DUDE. THERE'S ENOUGH CARROTS FOR US AND THE RABBITS IN THE NEIGHBORHOOD!
OKAY, COWGIRLS AND COWBOYS! LET'S GIDDYAP OUR HORSES AND GRILL THESE DINNERS OVER THE CAMPFIRE!

THIS IS SO GOOD! EVEN WITH VEGGIES. I WANT TO DO THIS AT HOME.

IF YOU WANT VEGGIES, MOM WILL BE ALL IN. HEY, WHERE'S SOFIA?

SOOOOFIIIIA! TIME TO EAT!

JUST A SECOND!

"WE ALL KNOW SOFIA LOVES TO COOK AND SHE'S SO GOOD AT ART. YOU NEVER KNOW HOW SHE'LL USE HER IMAGINATION...

READY TO GO BUGGY?

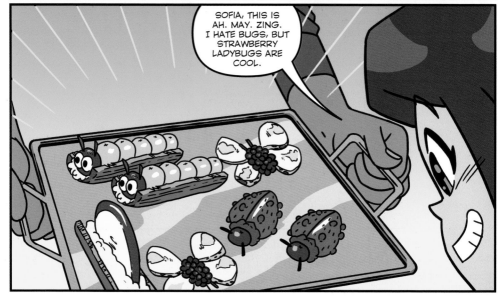

SOFIA, THIS IS AH. MAY. ZING. I HATE BUGS, BUT STRAWBERRY LADYBUGS ARE COOL.

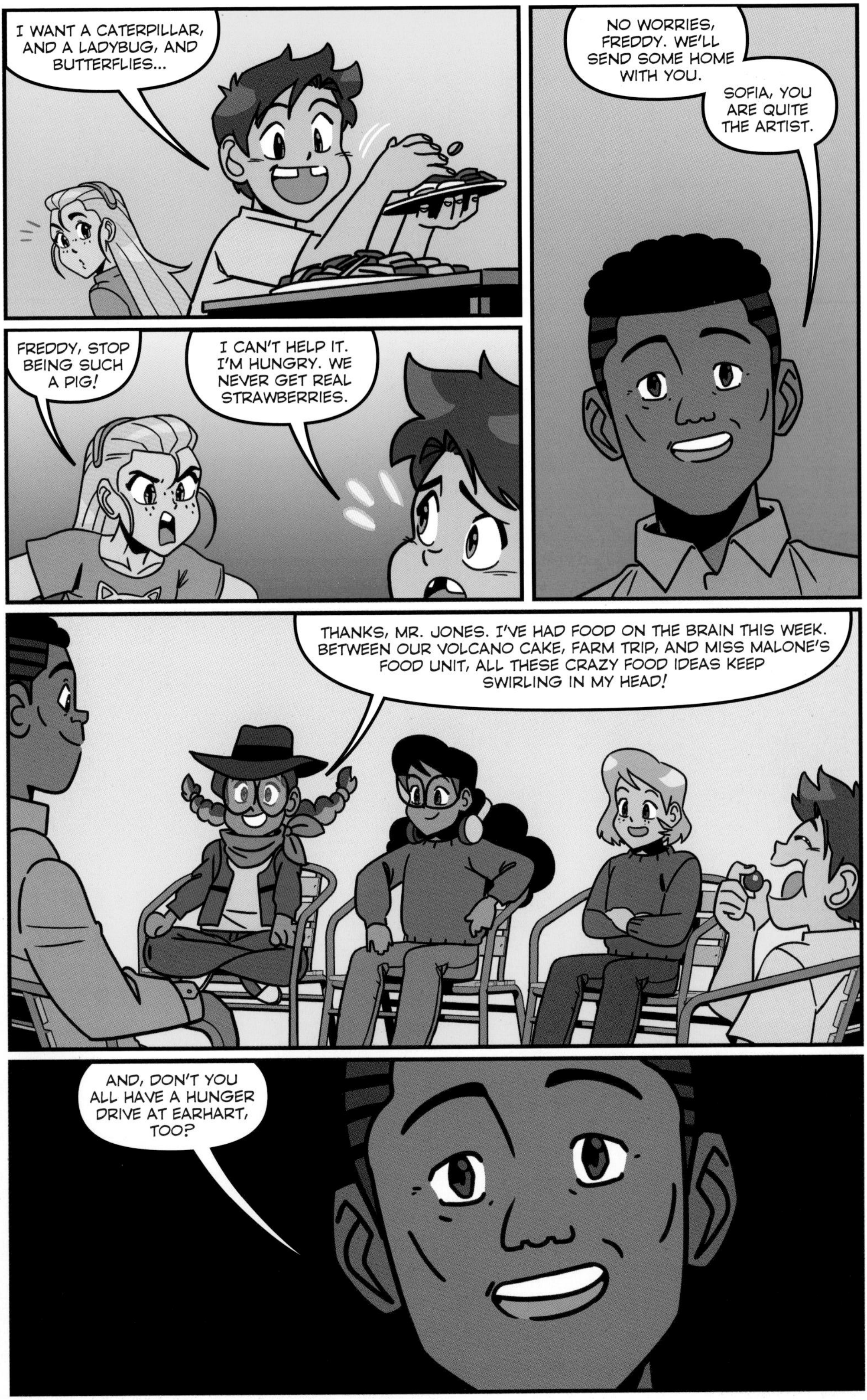
I WANT A CATERPILLAR, AND A LADYBUG, AND BUTTERFLIES...
NO WORRIES, FREDDY. WE'LL SEND SOME HOME WITH YOU.
SOFIA, YOU ARE QUITE THE ARTIST.
FREDDY, STOP BEING SUCH A PIG!
I CAN'T HELP IT. I'M HUNGRY. WE NEVER GET REAL STRAWBERRIES.
THANKS, MR. JONES. I'VE HAD FOOD ON THE BRAIN THIS WEEK. BETWEEN OUR VOLCANO CAKE, FARM TRIP, AND MISS MALONE'S FOOD UNIT, ALL THESE CRAZY FOOD IDEAS KEEP SWIRLING IN MY HEAD!
AND, DON'T YOU ALL HAVE A HUNGER DRIVE AT EARHART, TOO?

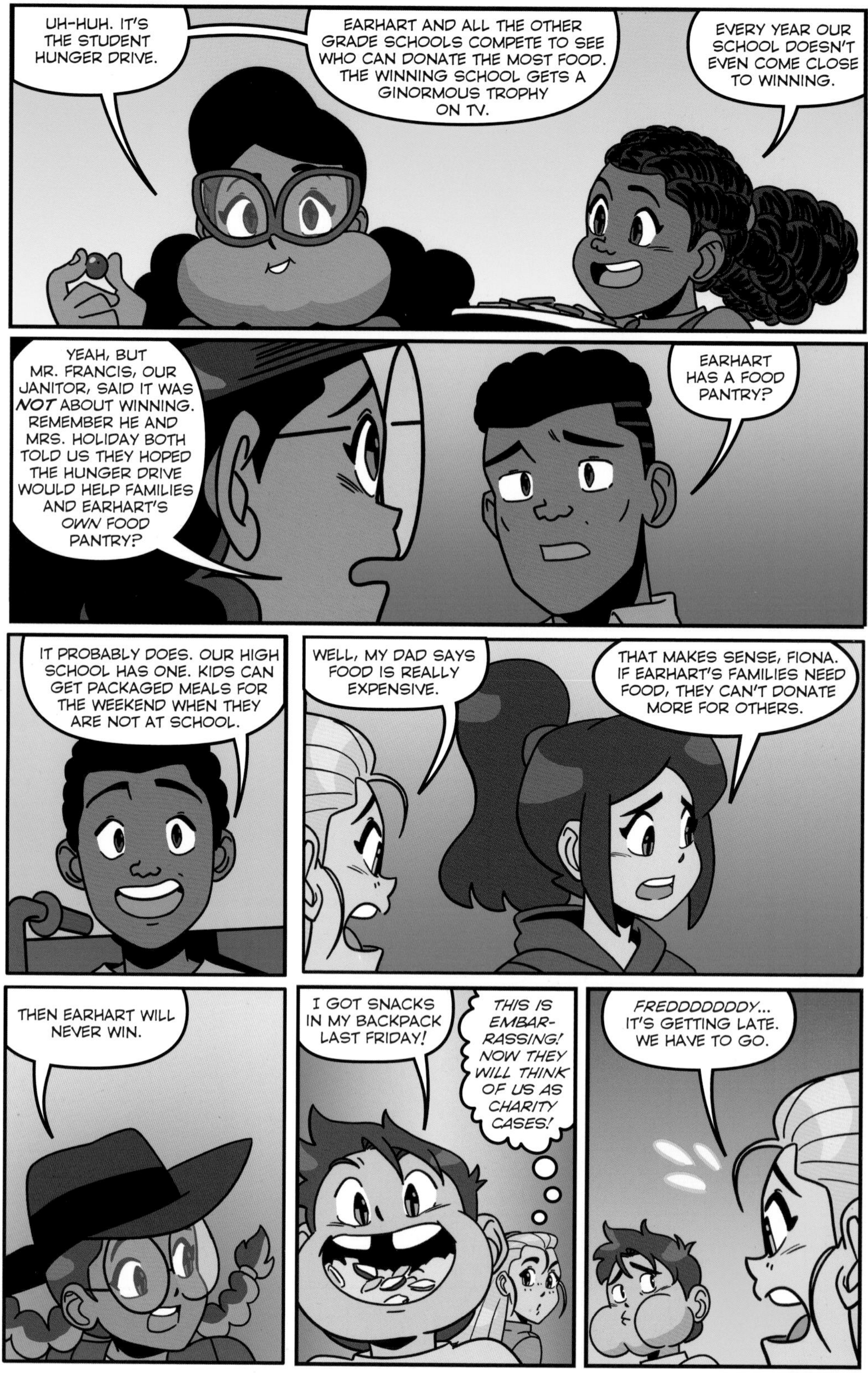
UH-HUH. IT'S THE STUDENT HUNGER DRIVE.
EARHART AND ALL THE OTHER GRADE SCHOOLS COMPETE TO SEE WHO CAN DONATE THE MOST FOOD. THE WINNING SCHOOL GETS A GINORMOUS TROPHY ON TV.
EVERY YEAR OUR SCHOOL DOESN'T EVEN COME CLOSE TO WINNING.
YEAH, BUT MR. FRANCIS, OUR JANITOR, SAID IT WAS *NOT* ABOUT WINNING. REMEMBER HE AND MRS. HOLIDAY BOTH TOLD US THEY HOPED THE HUNGER DRIVE WOULD HELP FAMILIES AND EARHART'S *OWN* FOOD PANTRY?
EARHART HAS A FOOD PANTRY?
IT PROBABLY DOES. OUR HIGH SCHOOL HAS ONE. KIDS CAN GET PACKAGED MEALS FOR THE WEEKEND WHEN THEY ARE NOT AT SCHOOL.
WELL, MY DAD SAYS FOOD IS REALLY EXPENSIVE.
THAT MAKES SENSE, FIONA. IF EARHART'S FAMILIES NEED FOOD, THEY CAN'T DONATE MORE FOR OTHERS.
THEN EARHART WILL NEVER WIN.
I GOT SNACKS IN MY BACKPACK LAST FRIDAY!
THIS IS EMBARRASSING! NOW THEY WILL THINK OF US AS CHARITY CASES!
FREDDDDDDDY... IT'S GETTING LATE. WE HAVE TO GO.

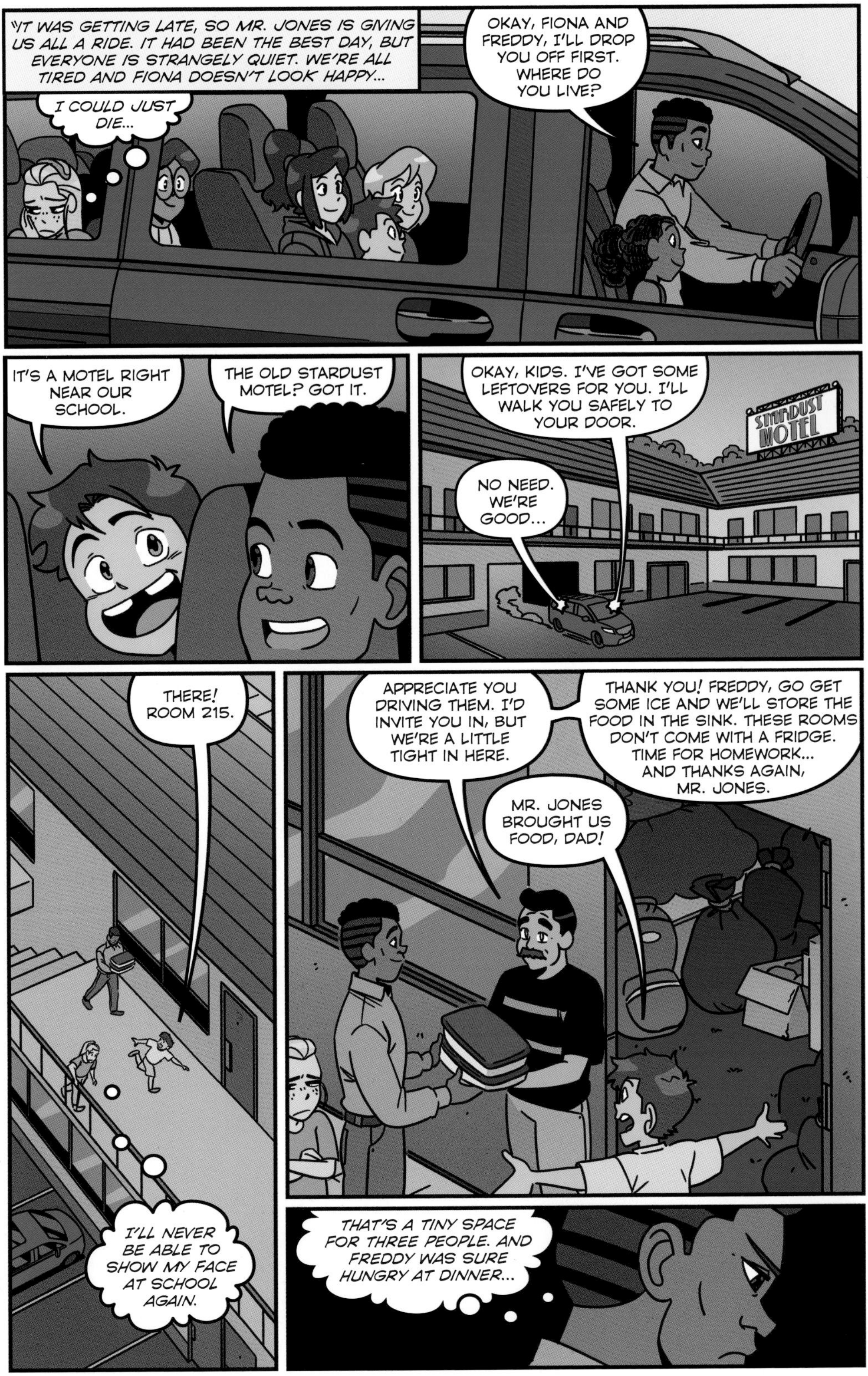

IT WAS GETTING LATE, SO MR. JONES IS GIVING US ALL A RIDE. IT HAD BEEN THE BEST DAY, BUT EVERYONE IS STRANGELY QUIET. WE'RE ALL TIRED AND FIONA DOESN'T LOOK HAPPY...
OKAY, FIONA AND FREDDY, I'LL DROP YOU OFF FIRST. WHERE DO YOU LIVE?
I COULD JUST DIE...
IT'S A MOTEL RIGHT NEAR OUR SCHOOL.
THE OLD STARDUST MOTEL? GOT IT.
OKAY, KIDS. I'VE GOT SOME LEFTOVERS FOR YOU. I'LL WALK YOU SAFELY TO YOUR DOOR.
STARDUST MOTEL
NO NEED. WE'RE GOOD...
THERE! ROOM 215.
I'LL NEVER BE ABLE TO SHOW MY FACE AT SCHOOL AGAIN.
APPRECIATE YOU DRIVING THEM. I'D INVITE YOU IN, BUT WE'RE A LITTLE TIGHT IN HERE.
THANK YOU! FREDDY, GO GET SOME ICE AND WE'LL STORE THE FOOD IN THE SINK. THESE ROOMS DON'T COME WITH A FRIDGE. TIME FOR HOMEWORK... AND THANKS AGAIN, MR. JONES.
MR. JONES BROUGHT US FOOD, DAD!
THAT'S A TINY SPACE FOR THREE PEOPLE. AND FREDDY WAS SURE HUNGRY AT DINNER...

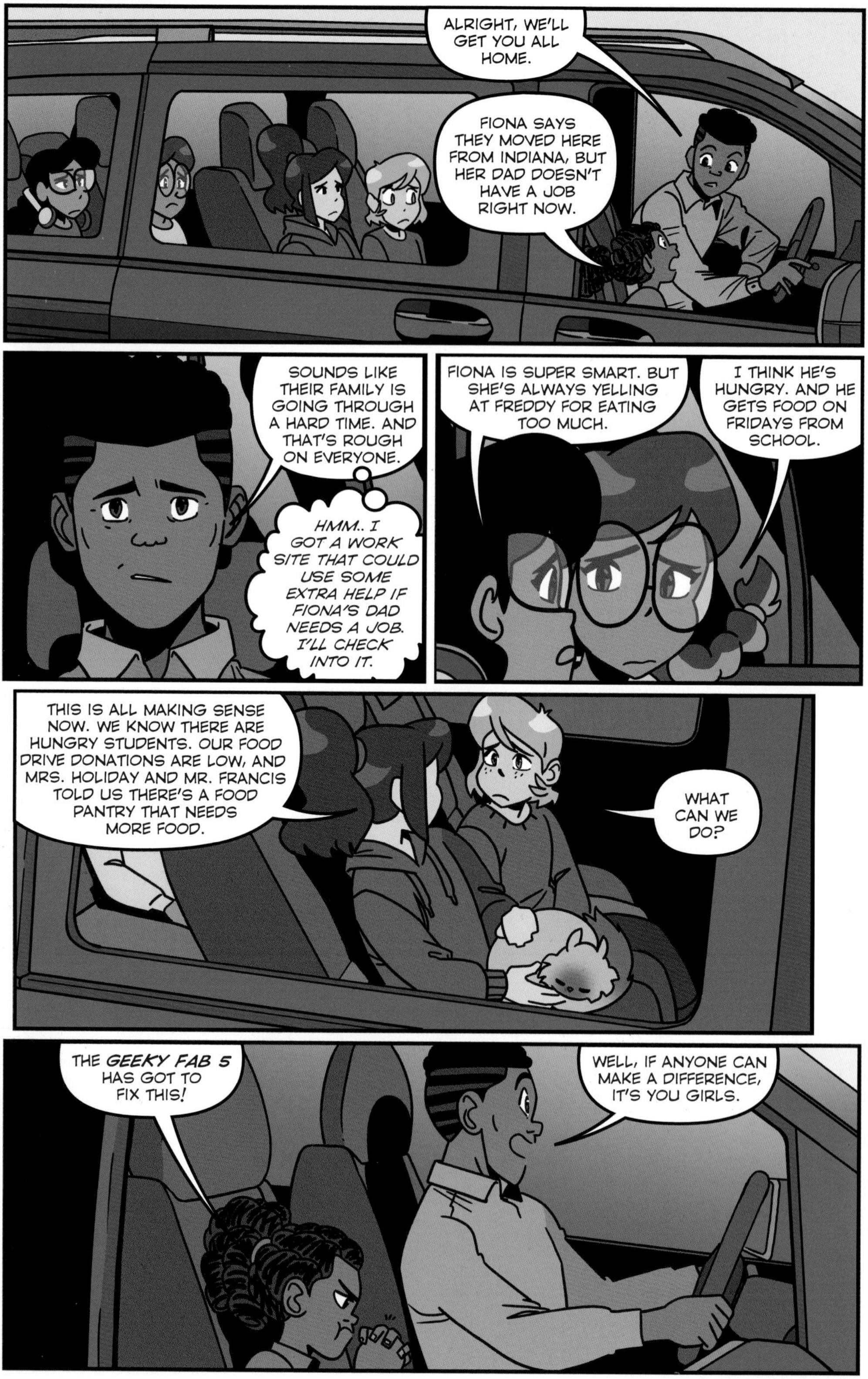

ALRIGHT, WE'LL GET YOU ALL HOME.
FIONA SAYS THEY MOVED HERE FROM INDIANA, BUT HER DAD DOESN'T HAVE A JOB RIGHT NOW.
SOUNDS LIKE THEIR FAMILY IS GOING THROUGH A HARD TIME. AND THAT'S ROUGH ON EVERYONE.
HMM.. I GOT A WORK SITE THAT COULD USE SOME EXTRA HELP IF FIONA'S DAD NEEDS A JOB. I'LL CHECK INTO IT.
FIONA IS SUPER SMART. BUT SHE'S ALWAYS YELLING AT FREDDY FOR EATING TOO MUCH.
I THINK HE'S HUNGRY. AND HE GETS FOOD ON FRIDAYS FROM SCHOOL.
THIS IS ALL MAKING SENSE NOW. WE KNOW THERE ARE HUNGRY STUDENTS. OUR FOOD DRIVE DONATIONS ARE LOW, AND MRS. HOLIDAY AND MR. FRANCIS TOLD US THERE'S A FOOD PANTRY THAT NEEDS MORE FOOD.
WHAT CAN WE DO?
THE *GEEKY FAB 5* HAS GOT TO FIX THIS!
WELL, IF ANYONE CAN MAKE A DIFFERENCE, IT'S YOU GIRLS.

CHAPTER SIX: VICTORY GARDENS

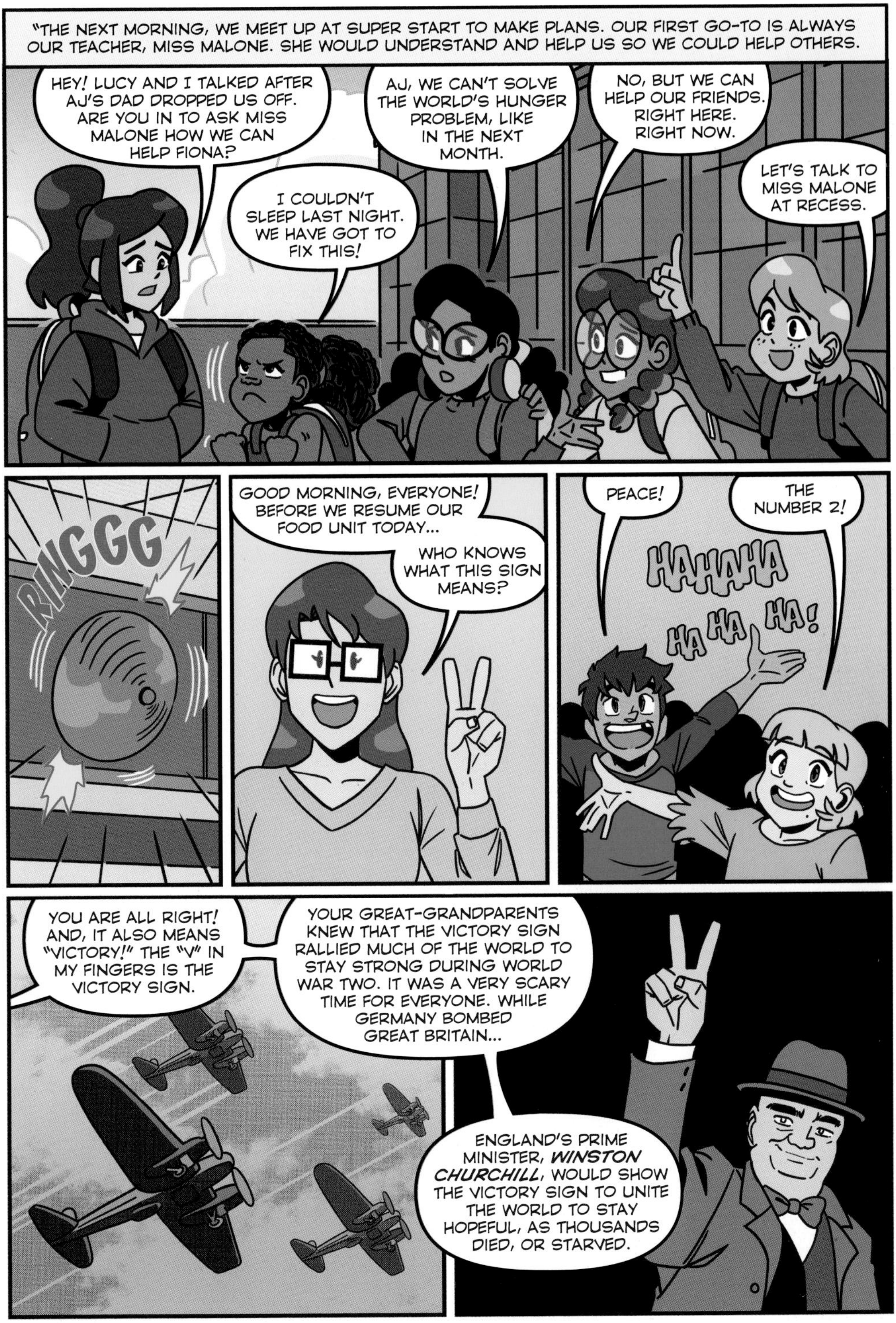

"THE NEXT MORNING, WE MEET UP AT SUPER START TO MAKE PLANS. OUR FIRST GO-TO IS ALWAYS OUR TEACHER, MISS MALONE. SHE WOULD UNDERSTAND AND HELP US SO WE COULD HELP OTHERS.
HEY! LUCY AND I TALKED AFTER AJ'S DAD DROPPED US OFF. ARE YOU IN TO ASK MISS MALONE HOW WE CAN HELP FIONA?
I COULDN'T SLEEP LAST NIGHT. WE HAVE GOT TO FIX THIS!
AJ, WE CAN'T SOLVE THE WORLD'S HUNGER PROBLEM, LIKE IN THE NEXT MONTH.
NO, BUT WE CAN HELP OUR FRIENDS. RIGHT HERE. RIGHT NOW.
LET'S TALK TO MISS MALONE AT RECESS.
RINGGG
GOOD MORNING, EVERYONE! BEFORE WE RESUME OUR FOOD UNIT TODAY...
WHO KNOWS WHAT THIS SIGN MEANS?
PEACE!
THE NUMBER 2!
HAHAHA
HA HA HA!
YOU ARE ALL RIGHT! AND, IT ALSO MEANS "VICTORY!" THE "V" IN MY FINGERS IS THE VICTORY SIGN.
YOUR GREAT-GRANDPARENTS KNEW THAT THE VICTORY SIGN RALLIED MUCH OF THE WORLD TO STAY STRONG DURING WORLD WAR TWO. IT WAS A VERY SCARY TIME FOR EVERYONE. WHILE GERMANY BOMBED GREAT BRITAIN...
ENGLAND'S PRIME MINISTER, WINSTON CHURCHILL, WOULD SHOW THE VICTORY SIGN TO UNITE THE WORLD TO STAY HOPEFUL, AS THOUSANDS DIED, OR STARVED.

HERE IN THE UNITED STATES, WE ALSO HELPED EUROPE WIN THE WAR. WOMEN WORKED FOR THE FIRST TIME IN FACTORIES THAT MADE TANKS.

AND MANY FAMILIES GREW VICTORY GARDENS!

HOW DO YOU FIGHT A WAR WITH TOMATOES?

HAHAHA HA HA HA!

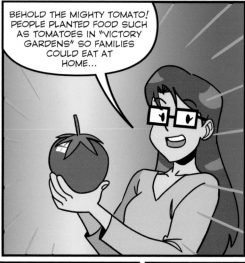

BEHOLD THE MIGHTY TOMATO! PEOPLE PLANTED FOOD SUCH AS TOMATOES IN "VICTORY GARDENS" SO FAMILIES COULD EAT AT HOME...

...WHILE OUR COUNTRY SHIPPED TONS OF CANNED FOOD THAT WOULDN'T SPOIL FOR THE SOLDIERS. THEY CARRIED THAT FOOD IN THEIR BACKPACKS WHILE FIGHTING.

VICTORY GARDENS. FOOD DRIVE. FIONA. I THINK I'VE GOT AN IDEA...

RINGGG

"IT WAS FINALLY RECESS..."

44

"... AND WE COULD TALK TO MISS MALONE ABOUT OUR HUNGRY FRIEND AND THE STUDENT HUNGER DRIVE."

WE ARE WORRIED ABOUT FIONA.

FIONA CALLED IN SICK TODAY, BUT IT DIDN'T SOUND SERIOUS.

WE TOOK HER AND FREDDY HOME LAST NIGHT. THEY LIVE IN A MOTEL. AND MRS. HOLIDAY AND MR. FRANCIS SAY WE'VE GOT A FOOD PANTRY THAT'S EMPTY.

PLEASE TELL US, WHAT IS HAPPENING AT OUR SCHOOL?

OKAY, GIRLS. I CANNOT TALK ABOUT SPECIFIC STUDENTS TO PROTECT THEIR PRIVACY. BUT I CAN SHOW YOU OUR FOOD PANTRY. FOLLOW ME.

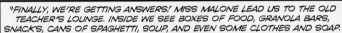

"FINALLY, WE'RE GETTING ANSWERS! MISS MALONE LEAD US TO THE OLD TEACHER'S LOUNGE. INSIDE WE SEE BOXES OF FOOD, GRANOLA BARS, SNACKS, CANS OF SPAGHETTI, SOUP, AND EVEN SOME CLOTHES AND SOAP."

GIRLS, OUR LOCAL FOODBANK SUPPLIES US WITH THIS FOOD. THE TEACHERS BUY OTHER SUPPLIES LIKE SOAP AND...

... TOOTHPASTE FOR OUR STUDENTS WHO DON'T HAVE THINGS WE USE EVERY DAY. SOME FAMILIES LIVE IN CARS--

OR IN MOTELS?

YES, MOTELS. EVERY FRIDAY, OUR SCHOOL NURSE OR TEACHERS GIVE NUTRITION CLUB MEMBERS MILK AND A SMALL BAG FULL OF FOOD, SO THEY CAN EAT THROUGH THE WEEKEND.

THEY DON'T HAVE TO SHARE IT WITH ANYONE.

MOST OF THESE SHELVES ARE EMPTY.

THIS ISN'T RIGHT, MISS MALONE. WE LIVE IN A TOWN SURROUNDED BY CORN! WE THROW FOOD AWAY!

NO, IT ISN'T RIGHT. BUT WHEN PARENTS ARE OUT OF WORK, OR DON'T MAKE ENOUGH MONEY TO PAY FOR A HOME OR FOOD, OUR STUDENTS SUFFER. IT'S HARD TO LEARN IF YOUR TUMMY IS GROWLING.

MISS MALONE, I'VE BEEN THINKING...

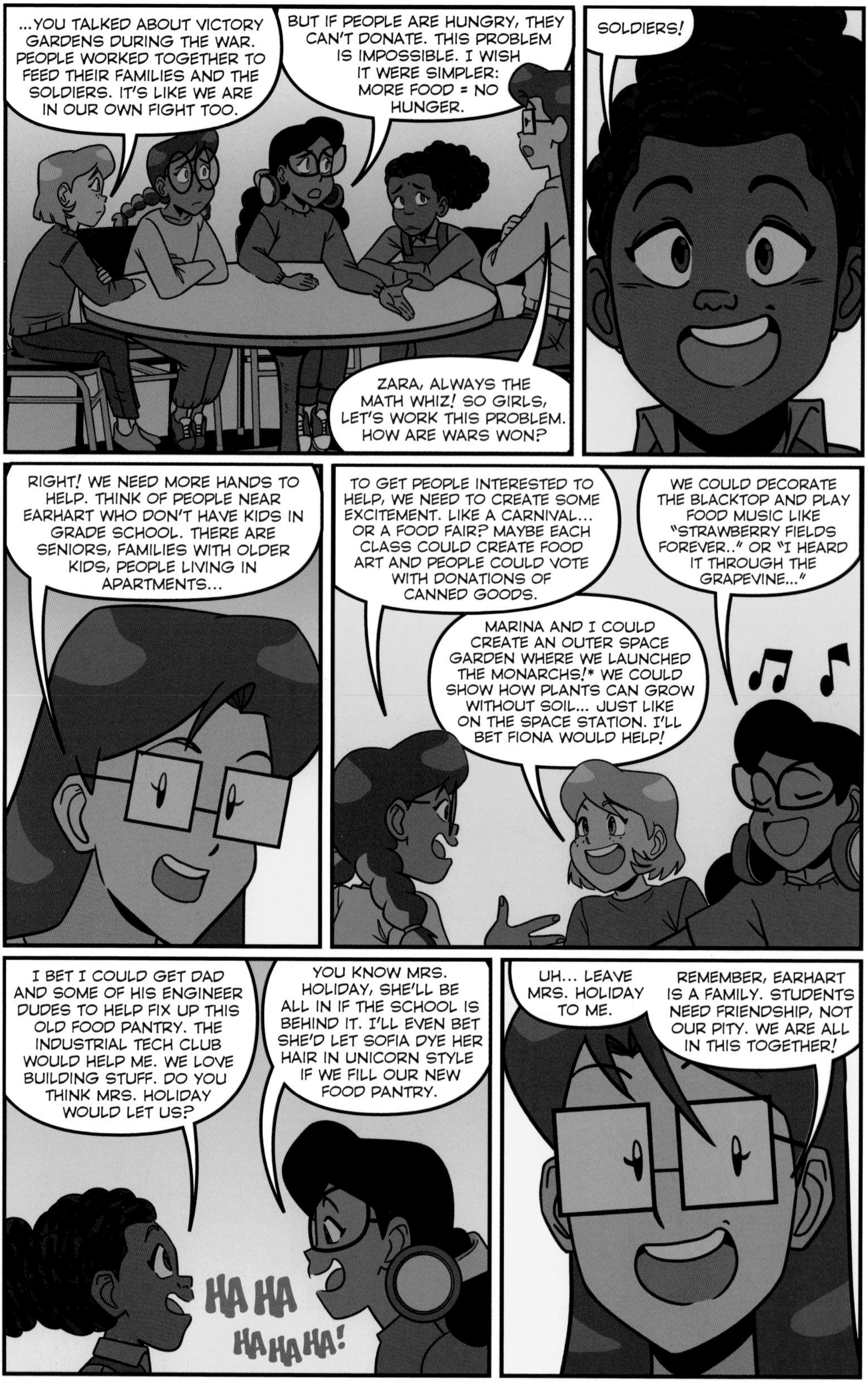
...YOU TALKED ABOUT VICTORY GARDENS DURING THE WAR. PEOPLE WORKED TOGETHER TO FEED THEIR FAMILIES AND THE SOLDIERS. IT'S LIKE WE ARE IN OUR OWN FIGHT TOO.
BUT IF PEOPLE ARE HUNGRY, THEY CAN'T DONATE. THIS PROBLEM IS IMPOSSIBLE. I WISH IT WERE SIMPLER: MORE FOOD = NO HUNGER.
ZARA, ALWAYS THE MATH WHIZ! SO GIRLS, LET'S WORK THIS PROBLEM. HOW ARE WARS WON?
SOLDIERS!
RIGHT! WE NEED MORE HANDS TO HELP. THINK OF PEOPLE NEAR EARHART WHO DON'T HAVE KIDS IN GRADE SCHOOL. THERE ARE SENIORS, FAMILIES WITH OLDER KIDS, PEOPLE LIVING IN APARTMENTS...
TO GET PEOPLE INTERESTED TO HELP, WE NEED TO CREATE SOME EXCITEMENT. LIKE A CARNIVAL... OR A FOOD FAIR? MAYBE EACH CLASS COULD CREATE FOOD ART AND PEOPLE COULD VOTE WITH DONATIONS OF CANNED GOODS.
WE COULD DECORATE THE BLACKTOP AND PLAY FOOD MUSIC LIKE "STRAWBERRY FIELDS FOREVER.." OR "I HEARD IT THROUGH THE GRAPEVINE..."
MARINA AND I COULD CREATE AN OUTER SPACE GARDEN WHERE WE LAUNCHED THE MONARCHS!* WE COULD SHOW HOW PLANTS CAN GROW WITHOUT SOIL... JUST LIKE ON THE SPACE STATION. I'LL BET FIONA WOULD HELP!
I BET I COULD GET DAD AND SOME OF HIS ENGINEER DUDES TO HELP FIX UP THIS OLD FOOD PANTRY. THE INDUSTRIAL TECH CLUB WOULD HELP ME. WE LOVE BUILDING STUFF. DO YOU THINK MRS. HOLIDAY WOULD LET US?
YOU KNOW MRS. HOLIDAY, SHE'LL BE ALL IN IF THE SCHOOL IS BEHIND IT. I'LL EVEN BET SHE'D LET SOFIA DYE HER HAIR IN UNICORN STYLE IF WE FILL OUR NEW FOOD PANTRY.
HA HA
HA HA HA!
UH... LEAVE MRS. HOLIDAY TO ME.
REMEMBER, EARHART IS A FAMILY. STUDENTS NEED FRIENDSHIP, NOT OUR PITY. WE ARE ALL IN THIS TOGETHER!

*SEE GEEKY FAB 5 #2 "MYSTERY OF THE MISSING MONARCHS."

CHAPTER SEVEN: FOOD FIGHT FOR FRIENDS

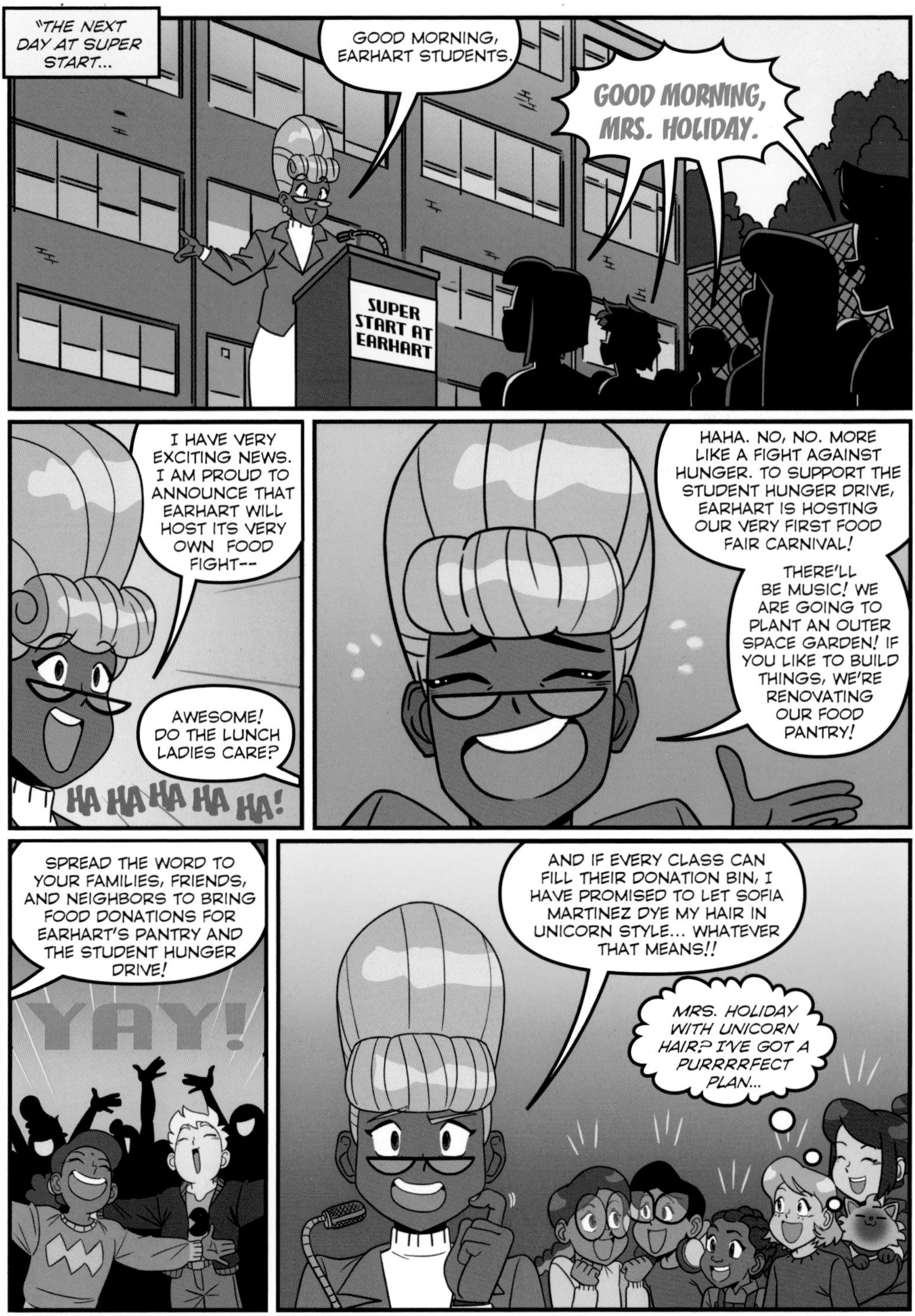

"THE NEXT DAY AT SUPER START...
GOOD MORNING, EARHART STUDENTS.
GOOD MORNING, MRS. HOLIDAY.
SUPER START AT EARHART
I HAVE VERY EXCITING NEWS. I AM PROUD TO ANNOUNCE THAT EARHART WILL HOST ITS VERY OWN FOOD FIGHT--
AWESOME! DO THE LUNCH LADIES CARE?
HA HA HA HA HA!
HAHA. NO, NO. MORE LIKE A FIGHT AGAINST HUNGER. TO SUPPORT THE STUDENT HUNGER DRIVE, EARHART IS HOSTING OUR VERY FIRST FOOD FAIR CARNIVAL!
THERE'LL BE MUSIC! WE ARE GOING TO PLANT AN OUTER SPACE GARDEN! IF YOU LIKE TO BUILD THINGS, WE'RE RENOVATING OUR FOOD PANTRY!
SPREAD THE WORD TO YOUR FAMILIES, FRIENDS, AND NEIGHBORS TO BRING FOOD DONATIONS FOR EARHART'S PANTRY AND THE STUDENT HUNGER DRIVE!
YAY!
AND IF EVERY CLASS CAN FILL THEIR DONATION BIN, I HAVE PROMISED TO LET SOFIA MARTINEZ DYE MY HAIR IN UNICORN STYLE... WHATEVER THAT MEANS!!
MRS. HOLIDAY WITH UNICORN HAIR? I'VE GOT A PURRRRFECT PLAN...

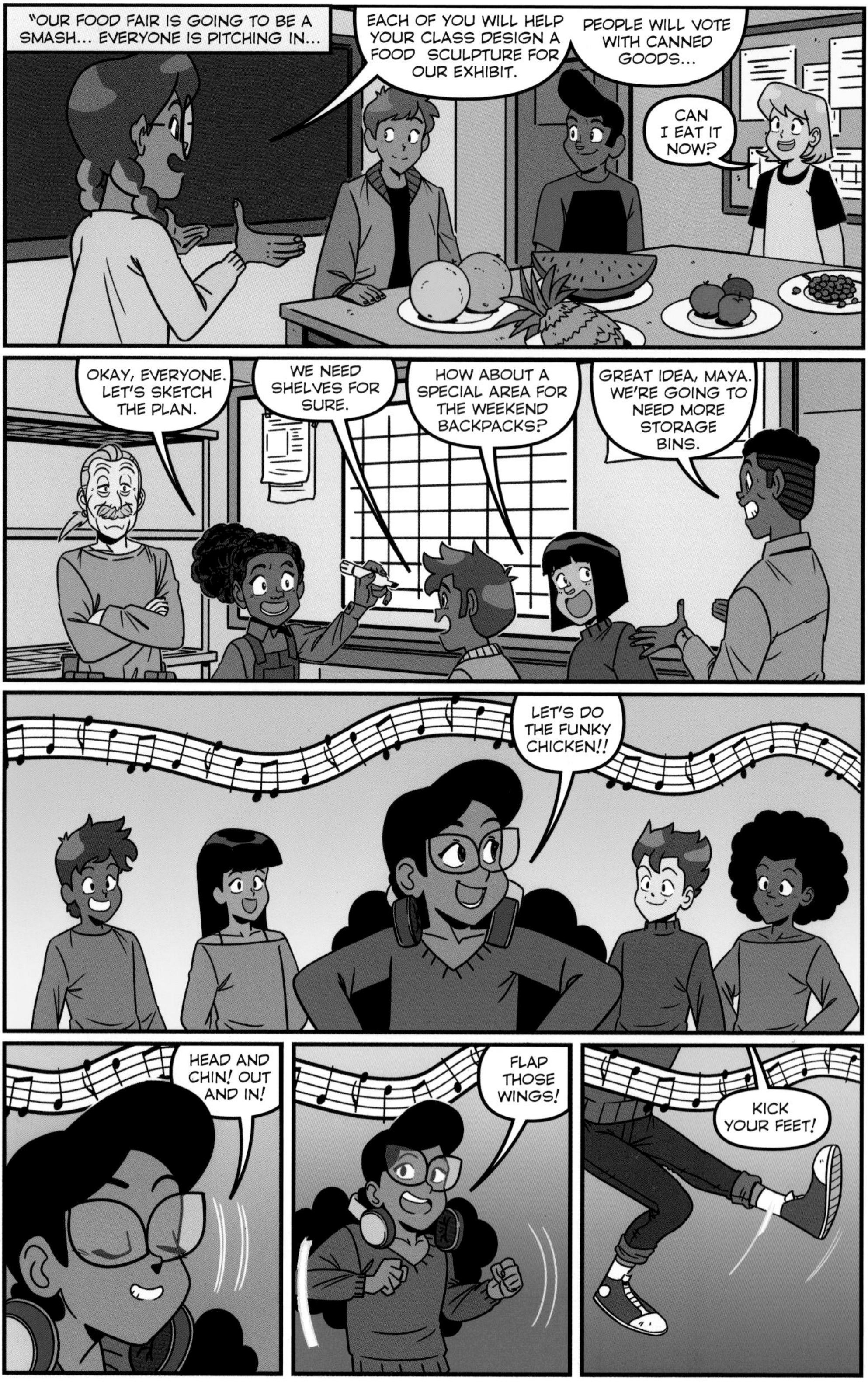
"OUR FOOD FAIR IS GOING TO BE A SMASH... EVERYONE IS PITCHING IN...
EACH OF YOU WILL HELP YOUR CLASS DESIGN A FOOD SCULPTURE FOR OUR EXHIBIT.
PEOPLE WILL VOTE WITH CANNED GOODS...
CAN I EAT IT NOW?
OKAY, EVERYONE. LET'S SKETCH THE PLAN.
WE NEED SHELVES FOR SURE.
HOW ABOUT A SPECIAL AREA FOR THE WEEKEND BACKPACKS?
GREAT IDEA, MAYA. WE'RE GOING TO NEED MORE STORAGE BINS.
LET'S DO THE FUNKY CHICKEN!!
HEAD AND CHIN! OUT AND IN!
FLAP THOSE WINGS!
KICK YOUR FEET!

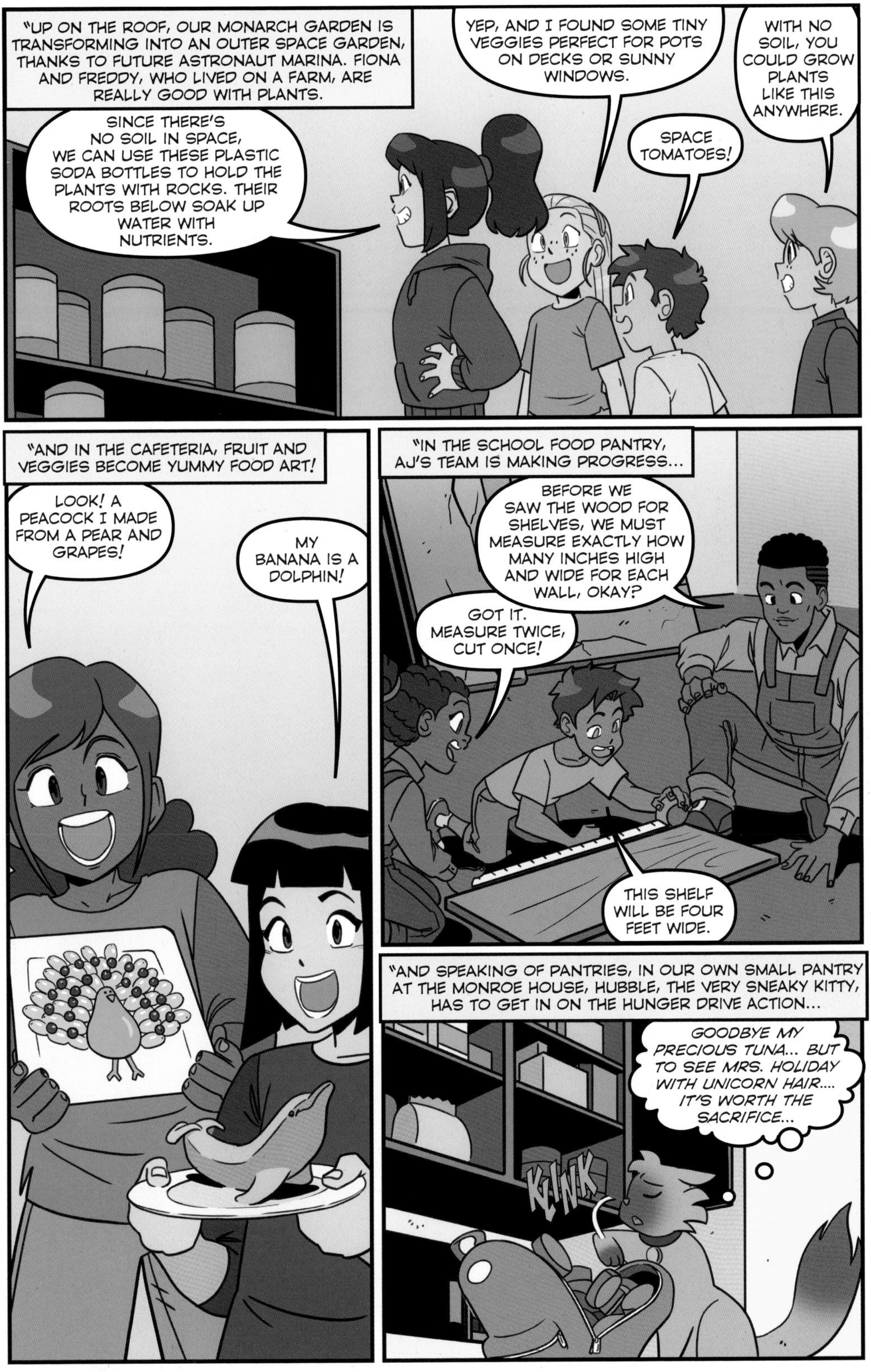
"UP ON THE ROOF, OUR MONARCH GARDEN IS TRANSFORMING INTO AN OUTER SPACE GARDEN, THANKS TO FUTURE ASTRONAUT MARINA. FIONA AND FREDDY, WHO LIVED ON A FARM, ARE REALLY GOOD WITH PLANTS.
YEP, AND I FOUND SOME TINY VEGGIES PERFECT FOR POTS ON DECKS OR SUNNY WINDOWS.
WITH NO SOIL, YOU COULD GROW PLANTS LIKE THIS ANYWHERE.
SINCE THERE'S NO SOIL IN SPACE, WE CAN USE THESE PLASTIC SODA BOTTLES TO HOLD THE PLANTS WITH ROCKS. THEIR ROOTS BELOW SOAK UP WATER WITH NUTRIENTS.
SPACE TOMATOES!
"AND IN THE CAFETERIA, FRUIT AND VEGGIES BECOME YUMMY FOOD ART!
LOOK! A PEACOCK I MADE FROM A PEAR AND GRAPES!
MY BANANA IS A DOLPHIN!
"IN THE SCHOOL FOOD PANTRY, AJ'S TEAM IS MAKING PROGRESS...
BEFORE WE SAW THE WOOD FOR SHELVES, WE MUST MEASURE EXACTLY HOW MANY INCHES HIGH AND WIDE FOR EACH WALL, OKAY?
GOT IT. MEASURE TWICE, CUT ONCE!
THIS SHELF WILL BE FOUR FEET WIDE.
"AND SPEAKING OF PANTRIES, IN OUR OWN SMALL PANTRY AT THE MONROE HOUSE, HUBBLE, THE VERY SNEAKY KITTY, HAS TO GET IN ON THE HUNGER DRIVE ACTION...
GOODBYE MY PRECIOUS TUNA... BUT TO SEE MRS. HOLIDAY WITH UNICORN HAIR.... IT'S WORTH THE SACRIFICE...
KLINK

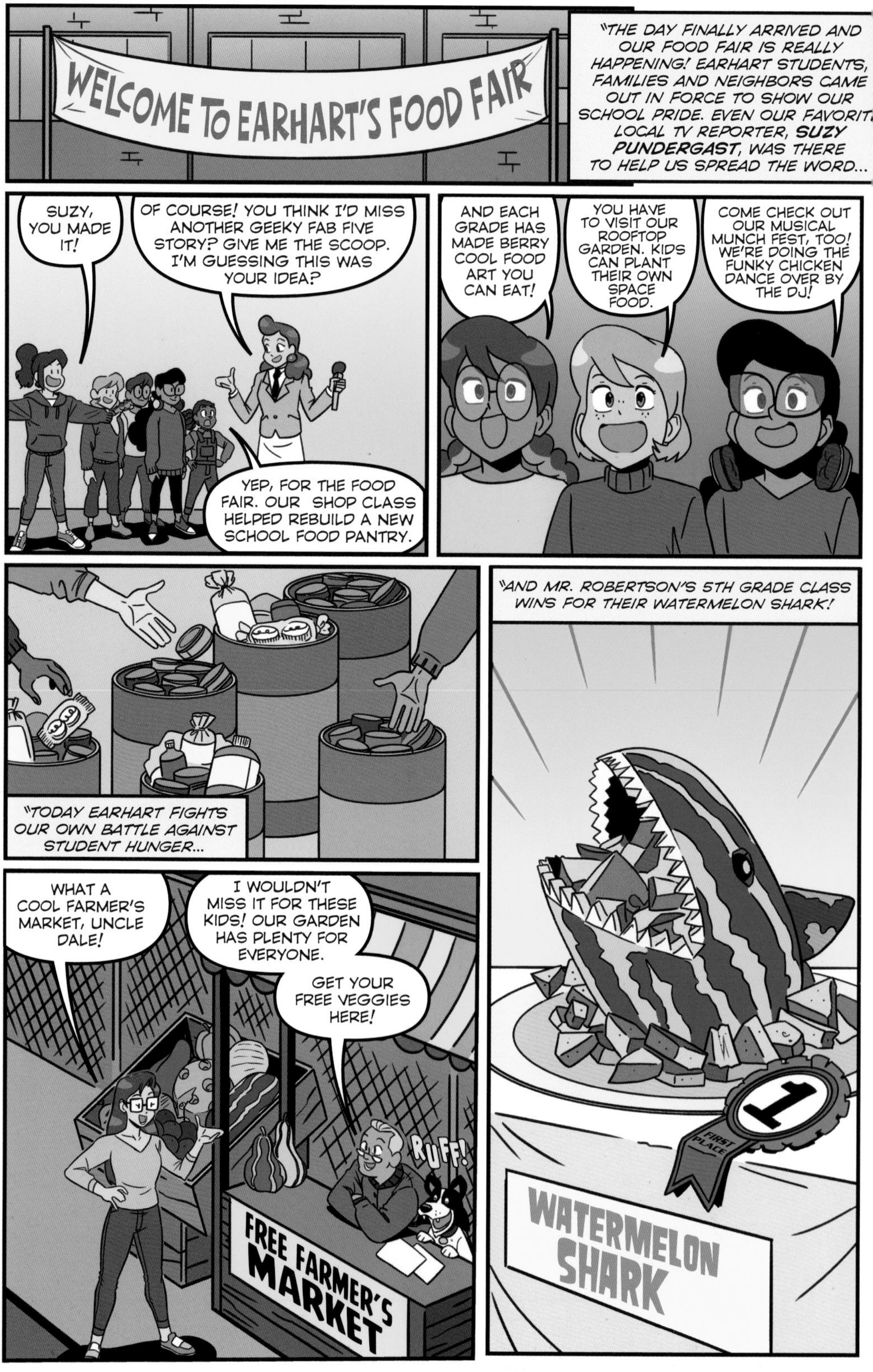
WELCOME TO EARHART'S FOOD FAIR
"THE DAY FINALLY ARRIVED AND OUR FOOD FAIR IS REALLY HAPPENING! EARHART STUDENTS, FAMILIES AND NEIGHBORS CAME OUT IN FORCE TO SHOW OUR SCHOOL PRIDE. EVEN OUR FAVORIT LOCAL TV REPORTER, **SUZY PUNDERGAST**, WAS THERE TO HELP US SPREAD THE WORD...
SUZY, YOU MADE IT!
OF COURSE! YOU THINK I'D MISS ANOTHER GEEKY FAB FIVE STORY? GIVE ME THE SCOOP. I'M GUESSING THIS WAS YOUR IDEA?
YEP, FOR THE FOOD FAIR. OUR SHOP CLASS HELPED REBUILD A NEW SCHOOL FOOD PANTRY.
AND EACH GRADE HAS MADE BERRY COOL FOOD ART YOU CAN EAT!
YOU HAVE TO VISIT OUR ROOFTOP GARDEN. KIDS CAN PLANT THEIR OWN SPACE FOOD.
COME CHECK OUT OUR MUSICAL MUNCH FEST, TOO! WE'RE DOING THE FUNKY CHICKEN DANCE OVER BY THE DJ!
"TODAY EARHART FIGHTS OUR OWN BATTLE AGAINST STUDENT HUNGER...
"AND MR. ROBERTSON'S 5TH GRADE CLASS WINS FOR THEIR WATERMELON SHARK!
FIRST PLACE
1
WATERMELON SHARK
WHAT A COOL FARMER'S MARKET, UNCLE DALE!
I WOULDN'T MISS IT FOR THESE KIDS! OUR GARDEN HAS PLENTY FOR EVERYONE.
GET YOUR FREE VEGGIES HERE!
RUFF!
FREE FARMER'S MARKET

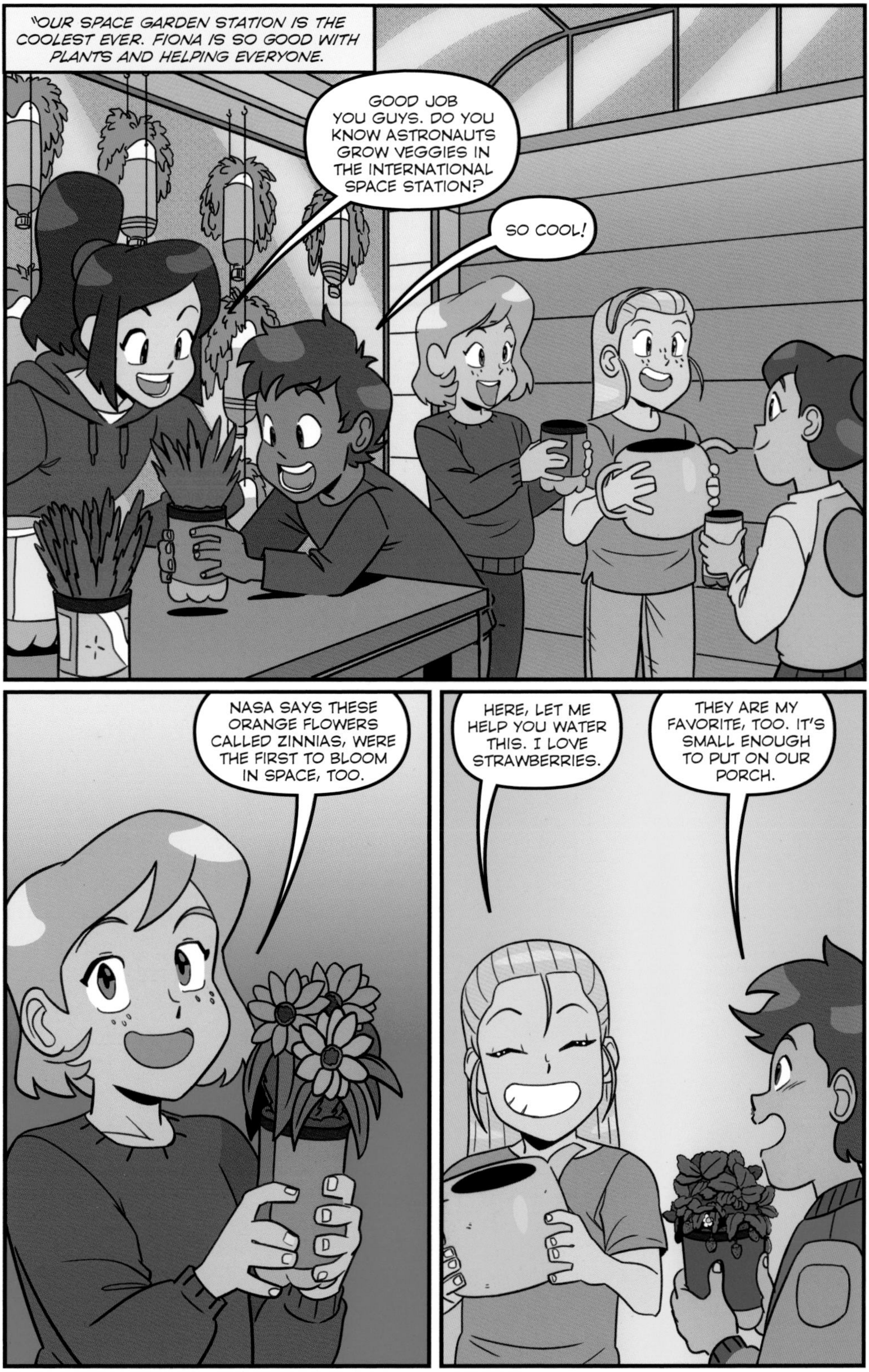
"OUR SPACE GARDEN STATION IS THE COOLEST EVER. FIONA IS SO GOOD WITH PLANTS AND HELPING EVERYONE.
GOOD JOB YOU GUYS. DO YOU KNOW ASTRONAUTS GROW VEGGIES IN THE INTERNATIONAL SPACE STATION?
SO COOL!
NASA SAYS THESE ORANGE FLOWERS CALLED ZINNIAS, WERE THE FIRST TO BLOOM IN SPACE, TOO.
HERE, LET ME HELP YOU WATER THIS. I LOVE STRAWBERRIES.
THEY ARE MY FAVORITE, TOO. IT'S SMALL ENOUGH TO PUT ON OUR PORCH.

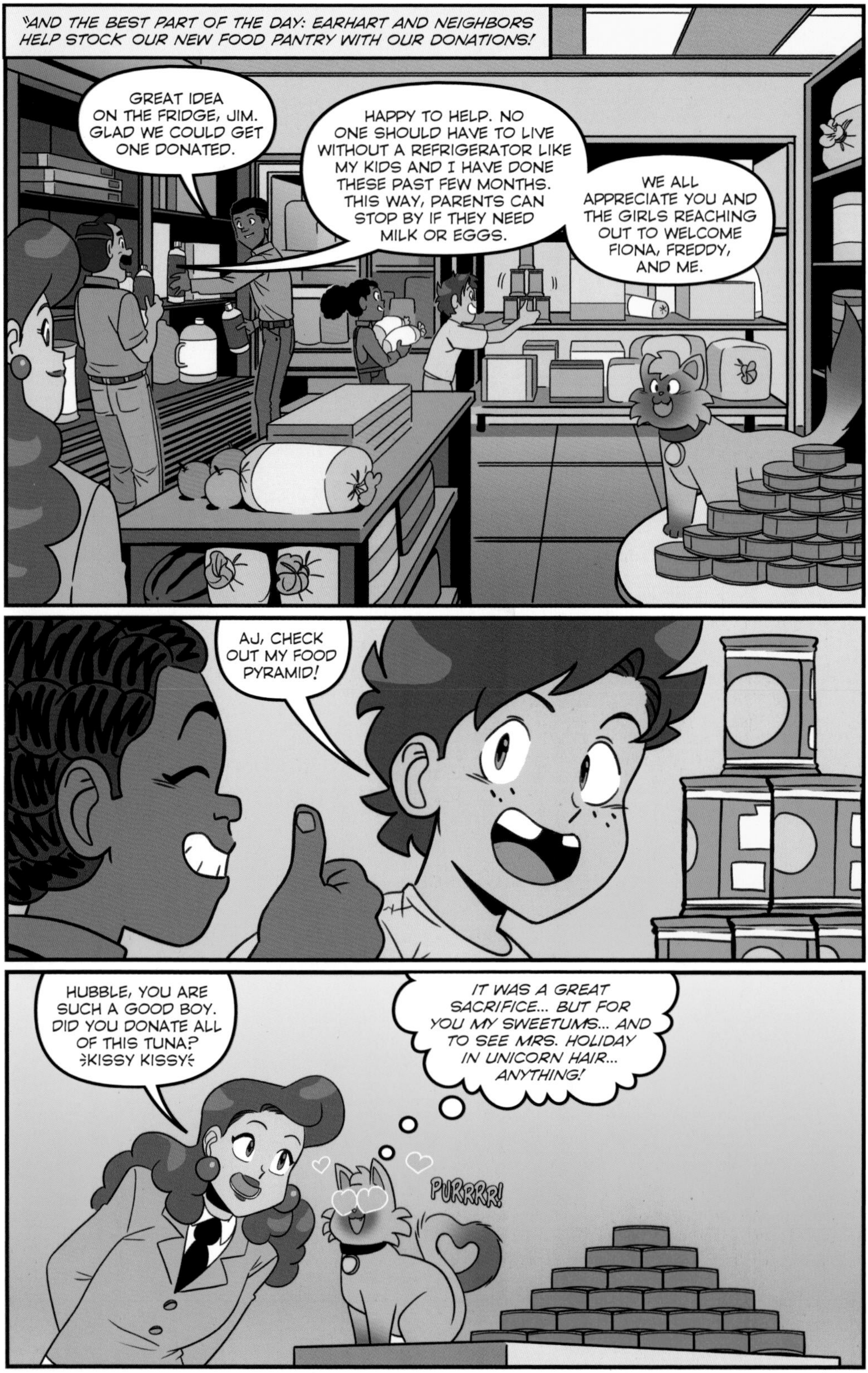
"AND THE BEST PART OF THE DAY: EARHART AND NEIGHBORS HELP STOCK OUR NEW FOOD PANTRY WITH OUR DONATIONS!
GREAT IDEA ON THE FRIDGE, JIM. GLAD WE COULD GET ONE DONATED.
HAPPY TO HELP. NO ONE SHOULD HAVE TO LIVE WITHOUT A REFRIGERATOR LIKE MY KIDS AND I HAVE DONE THESE PAST FEW MONTHS. THIS WAY, PARENTS CAN STOP BY IF THEY NEED MILK OR EGGS.
WE ALL APPRECIATE YOU AND THE GIRLS REACHING OUT TO WELCOME FIONA, FREDDY, AND ME.
AJ, CHECK OUT MY FOOD PYRAMID!
HUBBLE, YOU ARE SUCH A GOOD BOY. DID YOU DONATE ALL OF THIS TUNA? *KISSY KISSY*
IT WAS A GREAT SACRIFICE... BUT FOR YOU MY SWEETUMS... AND TO SEE MRS. HOLIDAY IN UNICORN HAIR... ANYTHING!
PURRRR!

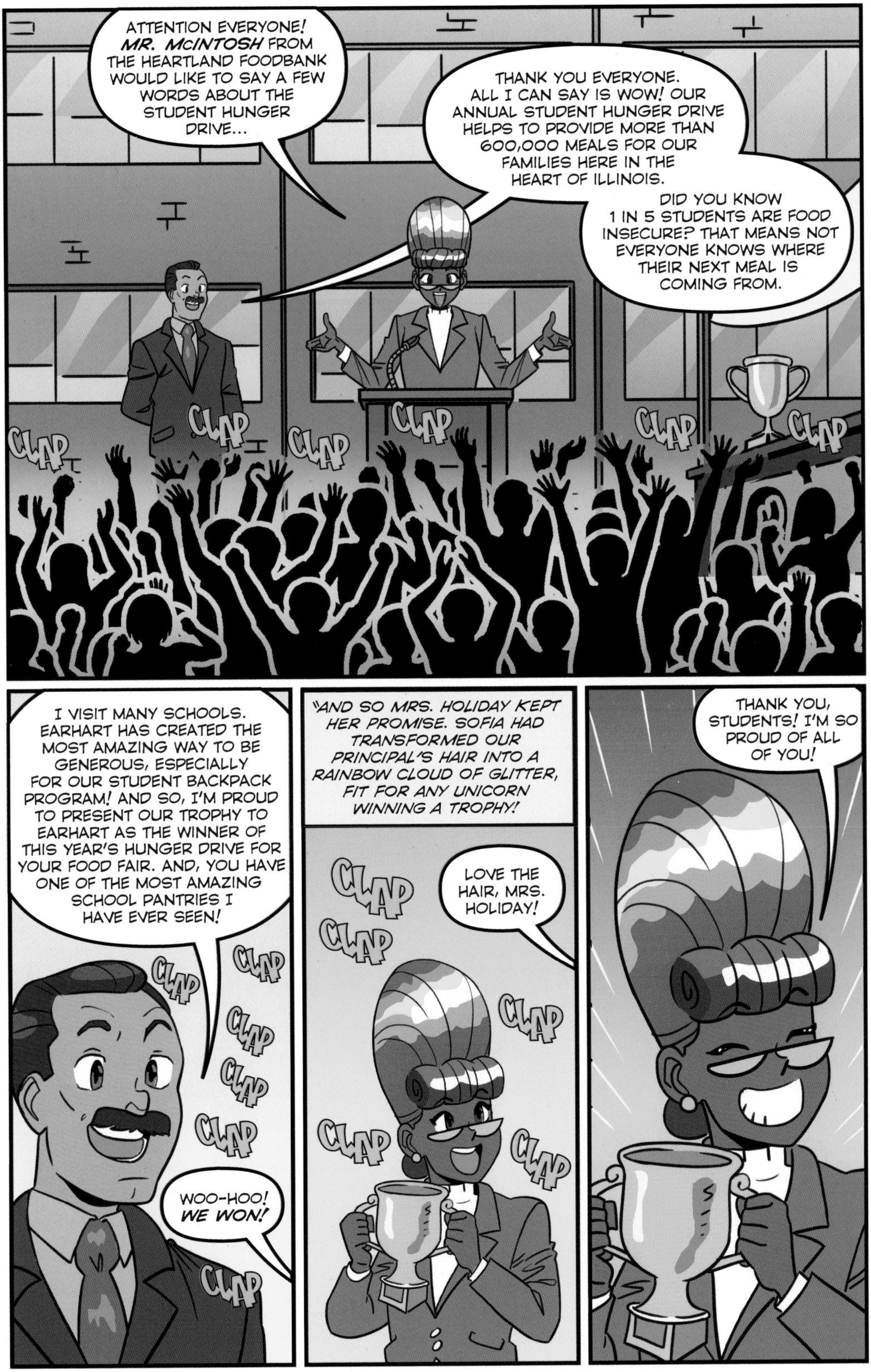
ATTENTION EVERYONE! **MR. McINTOSH** FROM THE HEARTLAND FOODBANK WOULD LIKE TO SAY A FEW WORDS ABOUT THE STUDENT HUNGER DRIVE...
THANK YOU EVERYONE. ALL I CAN SAY IS WOW! OUR ANNUAL STUDENT HUNGER DRIVE HELPS TO PROVIDE MORE THAN 600,000 MEALS FOR OUR FAMILIES HERE IN THE HEART OF ILLINOIS.
DID YOU KNOW 1 IN 5 STUDENTS ARE FOOD INSECURE? THAT MEANS NOT EVERYONE KNOWS WHERE THEIR NEXT MEAL IS COMING FROM.
CLAP CLAP CLAP CLAP CLAP CLAP
I VISIT MANY SCHOOLS. EARHART HAS CREATED THE MOST AMAZING WAY TO BE GENEROUS, ESPECIALLY FOR OUR STUDENT BACKPACK PROGRAM! AND SO, I'M PROUD TO PRESENT OUR TROPHY TO EARHART AS THE WINNER OF THIS YEAR'S HUNGER DRIVE FOR YOUR FOOD FAIR. AND, YOU HAVE ONE OF THE MOST AMAZING SCHOOL PANTRIES I HAVE EVER SEEN!
CLAP CLAP CLAP CLAP CLAP
WOO-HOO! **WE WON!**
CLAP
"AND SO MRS. HOLIDAY KEPT HER PROMISE. SOFIA HAD TRANSFORMED OUR PRINCIPAL'S HAIR INTO A RAINBOW CLOUD OF GLITTER, FIT FOR ANY UNICORN WINNING A TROPHY!
CLAP CLAP
LOVE THE HAIR, MRS. HOLIDAY!
CLAP CLAP CLAP
THANK YOU, STUDENTS! I'M SO PROUD OF ALL OF YOU!

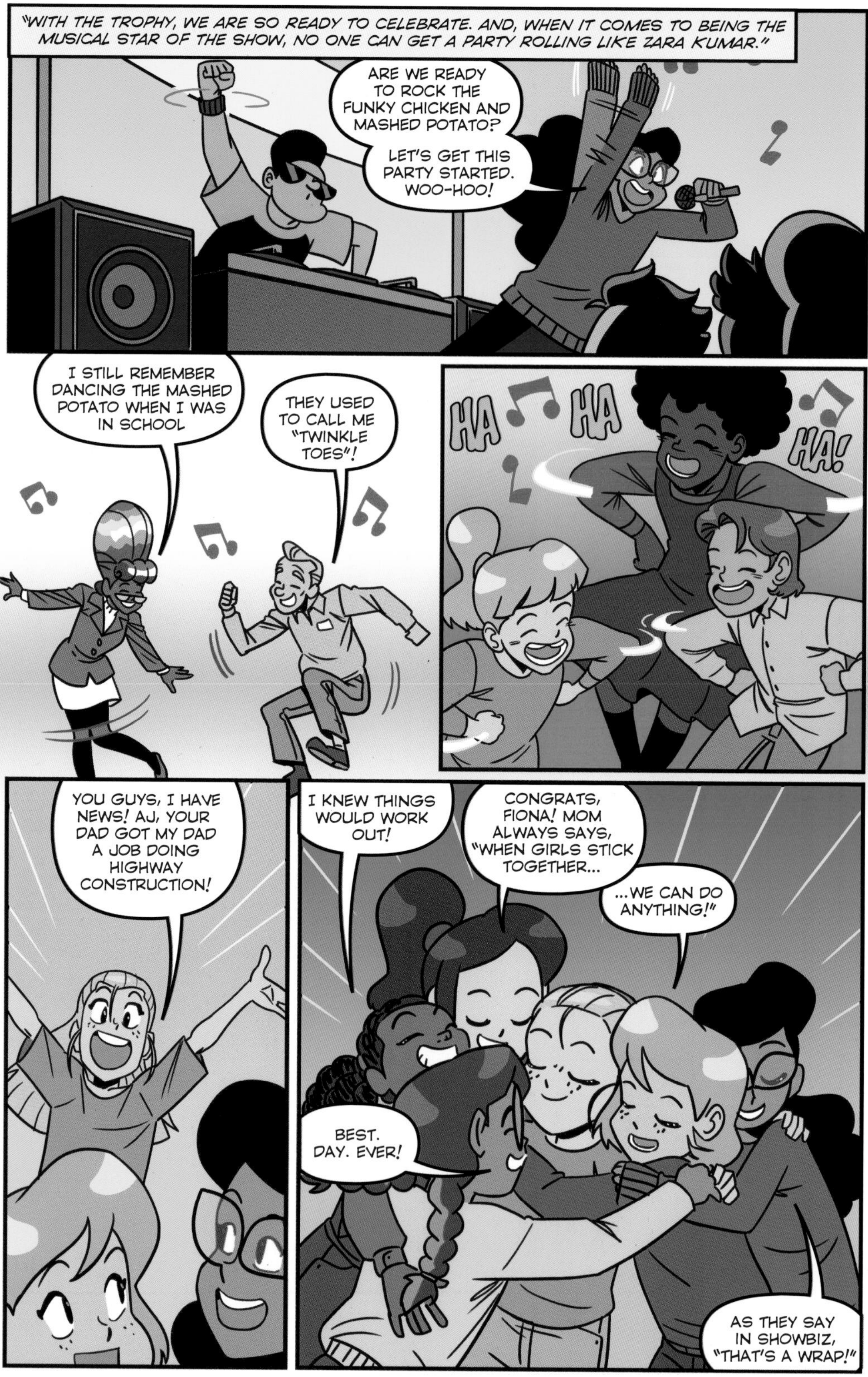
"WITH THE TROPHY, WE ARE SO READY TO CELEBRATE. AND, WHEN IT COMES TO BEING THE MUSICAL STAR OF THE SHOW, NO ONE CAN GET A PARTY ROLLING LIKE ZARA KUMAR."
ARE WE READY TO ROCK THE FUNKY CHICKEN AND MASHED POTATO?
LET'S GET THIS PARTY STARTED. WOO-HOO!
I STILL REMEMBER DANCING THE MASHED POTATO WHEN I WAS IN SCHOOL
THEY USED TO CALL ME "TWINKLE TOES"!
HA HA HA!
YOU GUYS, I HAVE NEWS! AJ, YOUR DAD GOT MY DAD A JOB DOING HIGHWAY CONSTRUCTION!
I KNEW THINGS WOULD WORK OUT!
CONGRATS, FIONA! MOM ALWAYS SAYS, "WHEN GIRLS STICK TOGETHER...
...WE CAN DO ANYTHING!"
BEST. DAY. EVER!
AS THEY SAY IN SHOWBIZ, "THAT'S A WRAP!"

WATCH OUT FOR PAPERCUTZ

Welcome to the farm-fresh fourth GEEKY F@B 5 graphic novel, "Food Fight for Fiona," by Lucy & Liz Lareau, our daughter/mother writing team, and Ryan Jampole, our award-winning artist, brought to you by Papercutz, the snack-loving folks dedicated to publishing great graphic novels for all ages. I'm Jim Salicrup, the Editor-in-Chief and fellow food-lover, here to talk a little about the subject matter of this graphic novel, hunger.

While the main goal of every Papercutz graphic novel is to offer you entertaining stories in comics form, quite often we manage to mix in material that may be educational, or in the case of "Food Fight for Fiona," thought-provoking and perhaps a bit more serious. For example, when AJ reflects, "Why is it that we are, like, surrounded by food every-where... corn, pigs, chickens, apples, but we still have to do a hunger food drive every year?" That's a good question, one we ask ourselves a lot.

When I was growing up in The Bronx, my family lived for several years at the Bronx River Housing Projects, a government-created housing develop-ment created for people who needed low-cost hous-ing until they could afford to pay market rents. At one point, I remember we ran out of food and couldn't afford to buy any more. My parents were terribly ashamed and embarrassed that it had come to that. I remember I had some coins I was saving to buy comicbooks, and I used that to buy a few White Castle hamburgers for my family that night.

It's easy for me to understand why Fiona feels so ashamed. Living in the projects and not having any food are things many insensitive kids will use to make fun of you. Fortunately for Fiona, the Geeky Fab 5 are not like that, and will do everything they can to help anyone in need. But Fiona never had any real reason to be ashamed, as being hungry was not her fault. Sometimes things happen—economic crisis, corporate downsizing, shifting consumer tastes, and so much more, such as a global pandemic—that cause people to lose their jobs or businesses, which can lead to losing homes and not having money to buy food.

Yet despite all these serious problems, there is still hope. All sorts of people in many differ-ent types of organizations are doing everything they can to help make things better. While I hope you're doing well, that you have plenty of food, are healthy, and have a safe place to live, I'm still very concerned about you. It is easy to get very depressed and filled with fear at times like these. The important thing is, no matter what you're facing, no matter how overwhelming it may seem, is not to give up.

As shown in "Food Fight for Fiona," schools have become a place that can help, and not by just offering food for the hungry. Schools offer the opportunity to learn about almost anything, and it's through gaining knowledge that you'll have the tools to help solve some of these problems we're all facing.

Over the years in this column, I've run a poem by Frank L. Stanton (1857-1927), and though it may seem corny and old-fashioned, and not address-ing how serious your particular problems may be, I truly believe in the spirit of it. It also seems to reflect the can-do attitude of the Geeky F@b 5. So, once again, I present this inspirational poem...

Keep A-Goin'

If you strike a thorn or rose,
Keep a-goin'!
If it hails or if it snows,
Keep a-goin'!
'Taint no use to sit an' whine
When the fish ain't on your line;
Bait your hook an' keep a-tryin'–
Keep a-goin'!
When the weather kills your crop,
Keep a-goin'!
Though 'tis work to reach the top,
Keep a-goin'!
S'pose you're out o' ev'ry dime,
Gittin' broke ain't any crime;
Tell the world you're feelin' prime-
Keep a-goin'!
When it looks like all is up,
Keep a-goin'!
Drain the sweetness from the cup,
Keep a-goin'!
See the wild birds on the wing,
Hear the bells that sweetly ring,
When you fell like singin', sing–
Keep a-goin'!

And if you keep a'goin to the next page, you'll find a Letter from Lucy, with her behind-the-scenes look at creating this graphic novel's story, and if you keep a-goin' past that, there's a preview of THE LOUD HOUSE #10 "The Many Faces of Lincoln Loud," which we hope you enjoy enough to pick up THE LOUD HOUSE graphic novels from Papercutz. And if you really keep a-goin', and staying safe, we hope you come back when GEEKY F@B 5 #5 is released, we're sure you'll enjoy it!

Thanks, Jim

STAY IN TOUCH!

EMAIL:	salicrup@papercutz.com
WEB:	papercutz.com
TWITTER:	@papercutzgn
INSTAGRAM:	@papercutzgn
FACEBOOK:	PAPERCUTZGRAPHICNOVELS
FAN MAIL:	Papercutz, 160 Broadway, Suite 700, East Wing, New York, NY 10038

Letter from LUCY LAREAU

Hi, everybody! When my mom and I started the Geeky F@b Five series, we always knew that tackling student hunger was an important issue because it is a more common problem that I thought.

When I was in grade school, I had no idea that some of my classmates would get food on Fridays to last them the weekend because they didn't have much food at home.

In my own school district and most schools in our community, school nurses keep a food pantry at the school. They hand out food on Fridays for kids so they don't go hungry over the weekend. The kids don't have to share their food with anyone. The meals consist of packaged and microwaveable foods such as cheese and crackers, soups, cereal, and granola bars. When I volunteered with my mom at the River Bend Foodbank, we and hundreds of others, helped fill these weekend "backpack" food packages. It sure seemed to me that wasn't much food to have for 6 meals, but our food bank only has so much food to feed thousands of families every week.

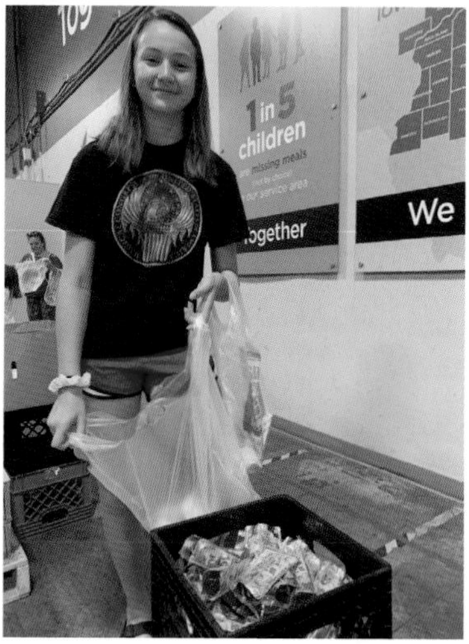
1 in 5
children
We

To help combat student hunger, one of the most exciting projects in our community is called the "The Student Hunger Drive." Schools compete to see which one can collect the most food and the winner gets a big party. In this book, we decided that the GF5 girls would focus on helping their new friend, Fiona, at their own school, Earhart Elementary.

Like Fiona, kids usually don't like talking about their hunger. So we created her little brother, Freddy, who loves food and can't stop talking about it! Fiona thinks he has a big mouth and is not ashamed at all. But what's important is that the GF5 wanted to help their friends and all kids who depend on their school food pantry!

I hope you enjoy this book! Does your school have a backpack program? To help maybe you and your friends could help donate time, food, money to your local food pantries to help students just like the Geeky F@b Five!

--Lucy

Special preview of THE LOUD HOUSE #10
"The Many Faces of Lincoln Loud"

"The Haunted House" by Derek Fridolfs – Writer; Max Alley – Artist; Amanda Rynda – Colorist; Wilson Ramos Jr. – Letterer

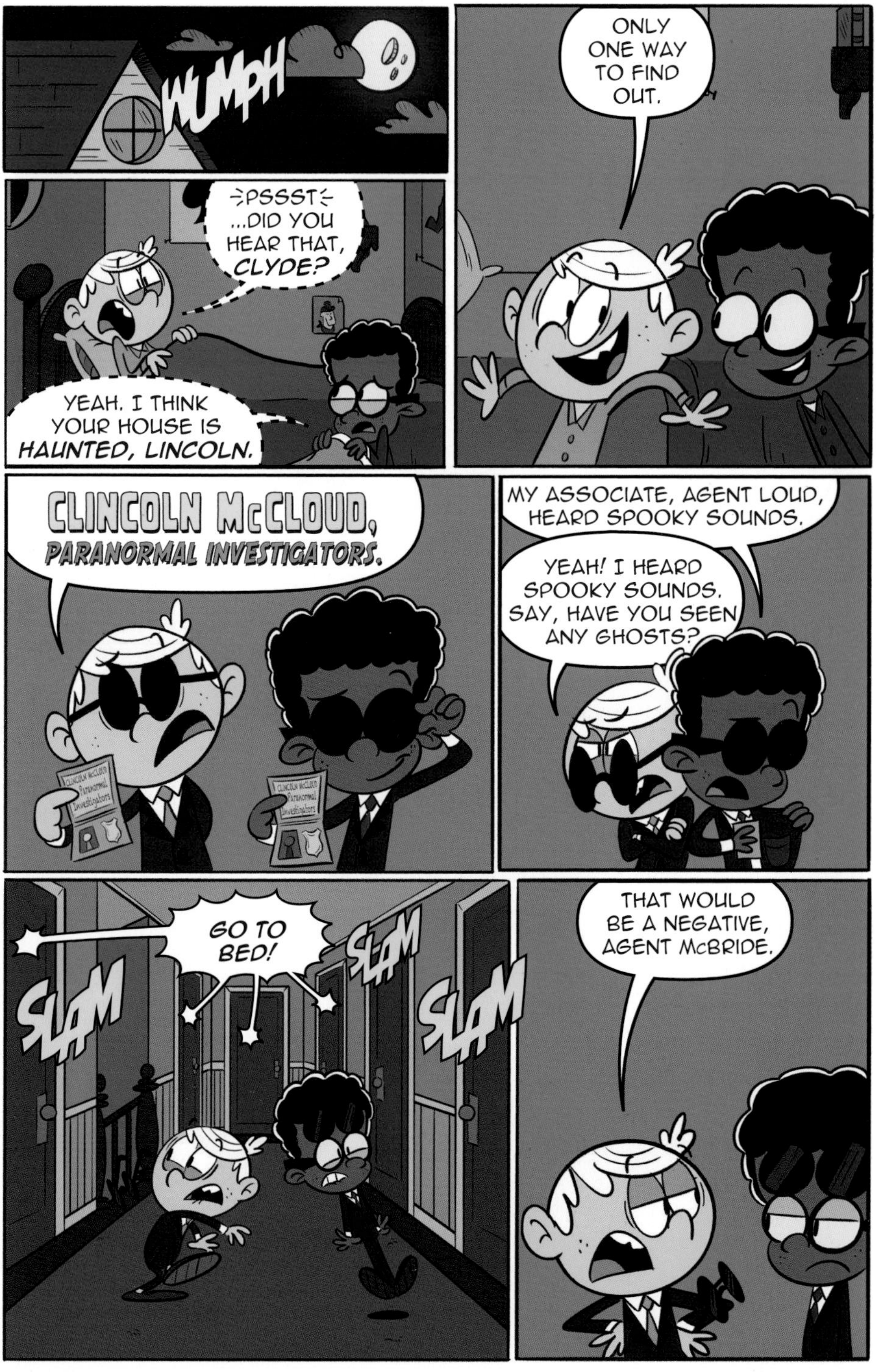
WUMPH
ONLY ONE WAY TO FIND OUT.
PSSST ...DID YOU HEAR THAT, CLYDE?
YEAH. I THINK YOUR HOUSE IS HAUNTED, LINCOLN.
CLINCOLN McCLOUD, PARANORMAL INVESTIGATORS.
MY ASSOCIATE, AGENT LOUD, HEARD SPOOKY SOUNDS.
YEAH! I HEARD SPOOKY SOUNDS. SAY, HAVE YOU SEEN ANY GHOSTS?
GO TO BED!
SLAM
SLAM
SLAM
THAT WOULD BE A NEGATIVE, AGENT McBRIDE.

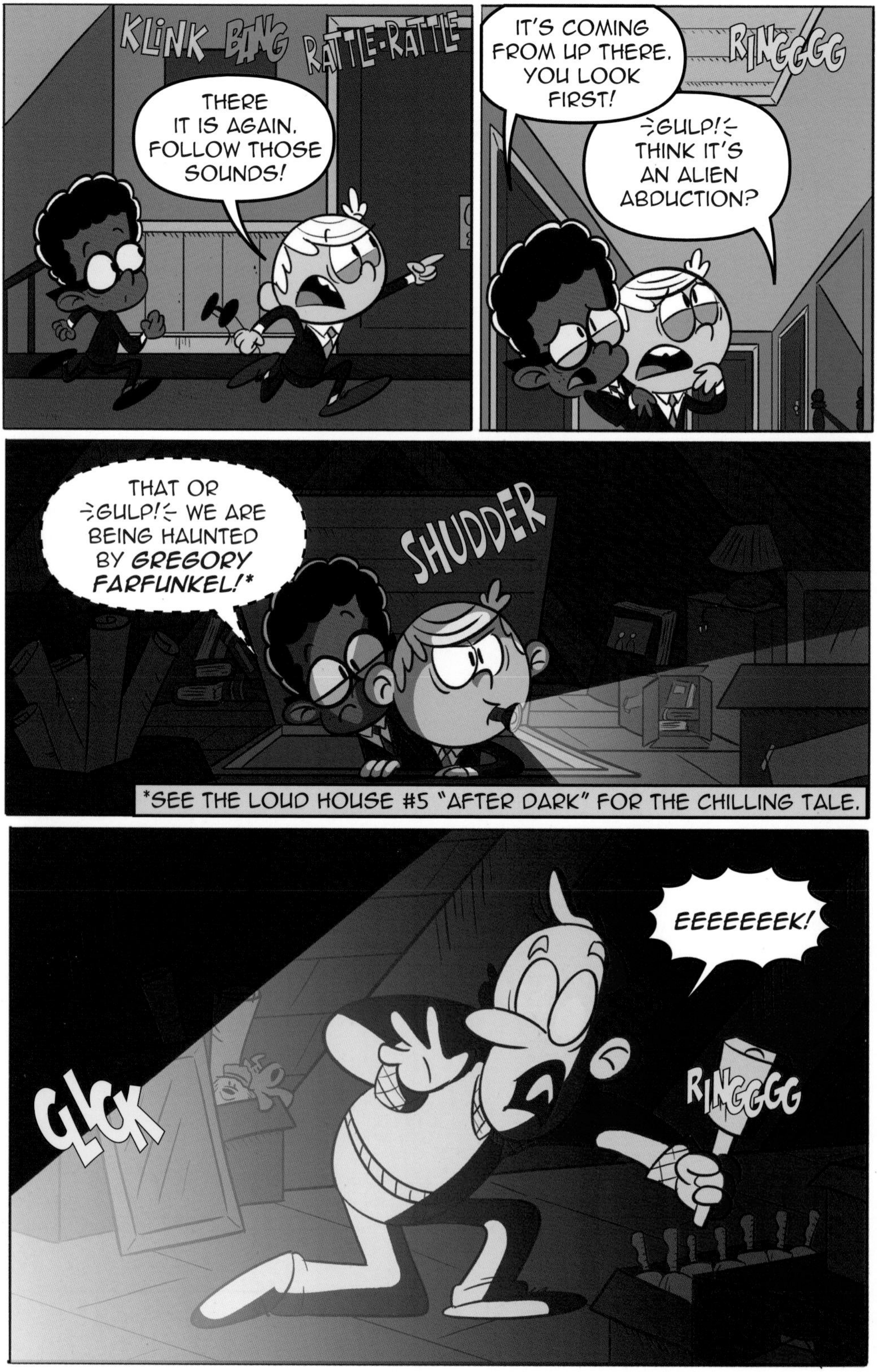
KLINK
BANG
RATTLE-RATTLE
THERE IT IS AGAIN. FOLLOW THOSE SOUNDS!
IT'S COMING FROM UP THERE. YOU LOOK FIRST!
RINGGGG
GULP! THINK IT'S AN ALIEN ABDUCTION?
THAT OR GULP! WE ARE BEING HAUNTED BY GREGORY FARFUNKEL!*
SHUDDER
*SEE THE LOUD HOUSE #5 "AFTER DARK" FOR THE CHILLING TALE.
EEEEEEEK!
CLICK
RINGGGG

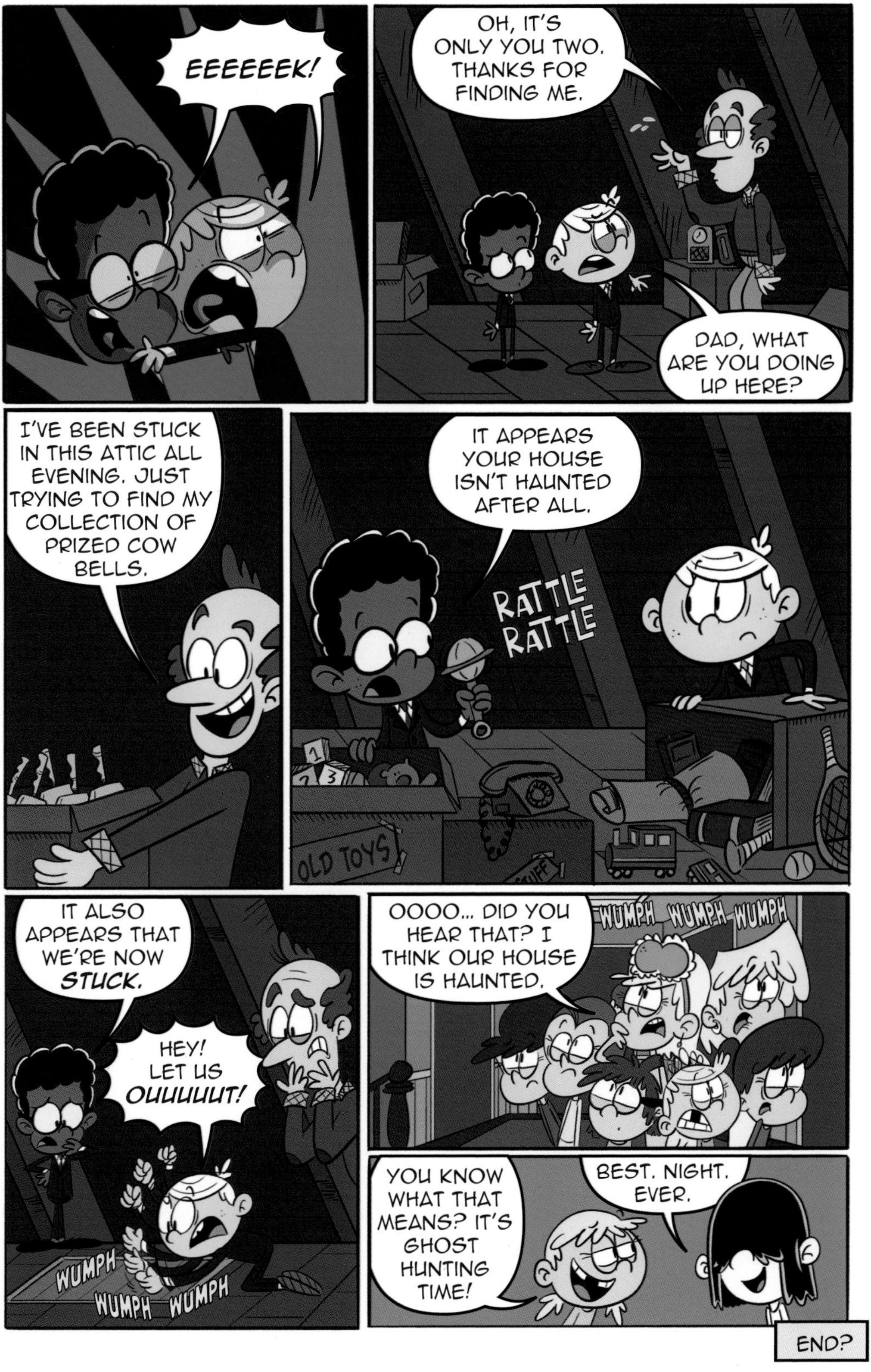
EEEEEEK!
OH, IT'S ONLY YOU TWO. THANKS FOR FINDING ME.
DAD, WHAT ARE YOU DOING UP HERE?
I'VE BEEN STUCK IN THIS ATTIC ALL EVENING. JUST TRYING TO FIND MY COLLECTION OF PRIZED COW BELLS.
IT APPEARS YOUR HOUSE ISN'T HAUNTED AFTER ALL.
RATTLE RATTLE
OLD TOYS
IT ALSO APPEARS THAT WE'RE NOW STUCK.
HEY! LET US OUUUUUT!
WUMPH WUMPH WUMPH
OOOO... DID YOU HEAR THAT? I THINK OUR HOUSE IS HAUNTED.
WUMPH WUMPH WUMPH
YOU KNOW WHAT THAT MEANS? IT'S GHOST HUNTING TIME!
BEST. NIGHT. EVER.
END?

"Lucy of Melancholia" by Caitlin Fein, Writer; Gizelle Orbino – Artist, Colorist; Wilson Ramos Jr. – Lettere

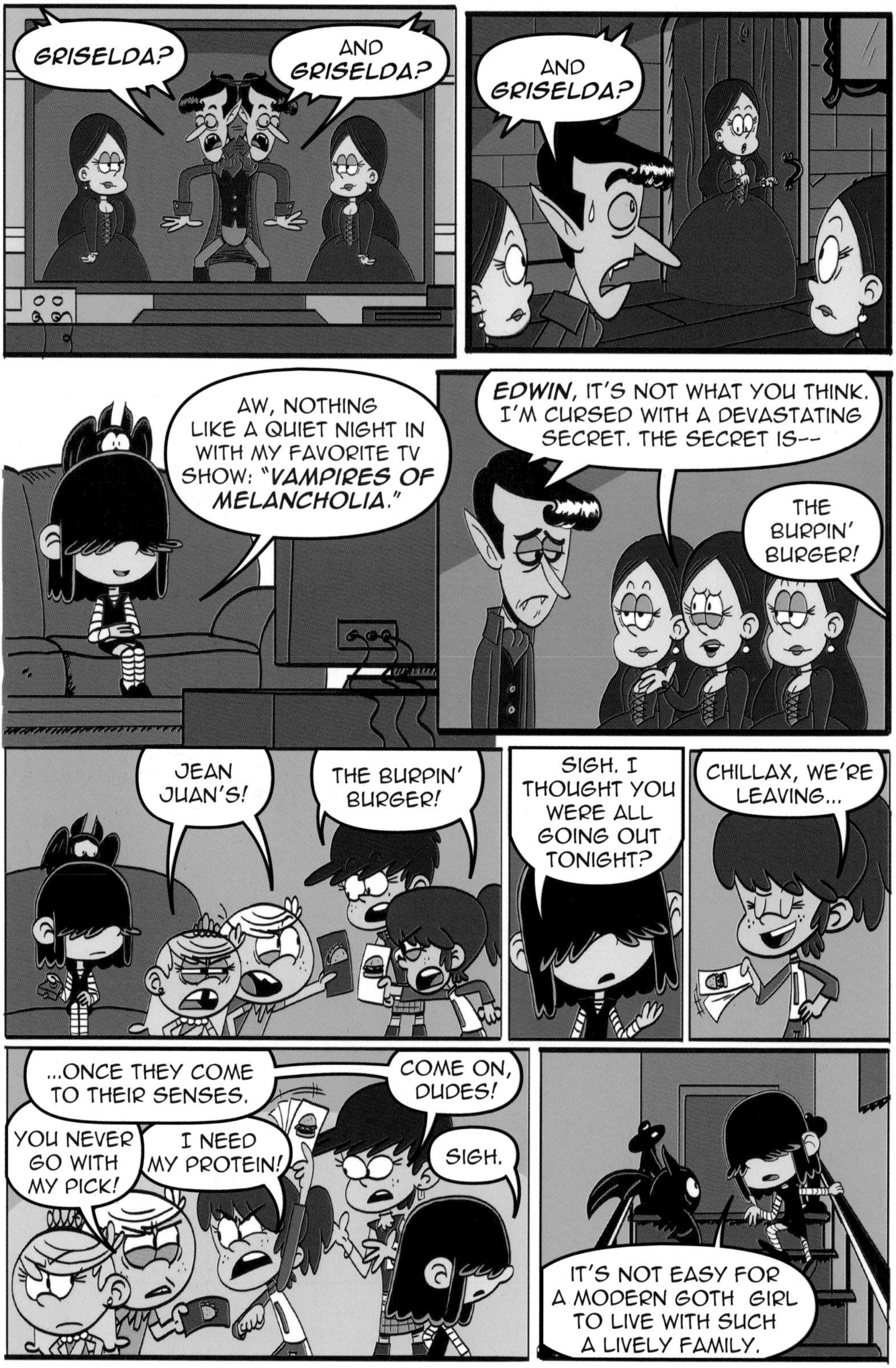

GRISELDA?
AND GRISELDA?
AND GRISELDA?
AW, NOTHING LIKE A QUIET NIGHT IN WITH MY FAVORITE TV SHOW: "VAMPIRES OF MELANCHOLIA."
EDWIN, IT'S NOT WHAT YOU THINK. I'M CURSED WITH A DEVASTATING SECRET. THE SECRET IS--
THE BURPIN' BURGER!
JEAN JUAN'S!
THE BURPIN' BURGER!
SIGH. I THOUGHT YOU WERE ALL GOING OUT TONIGHT?
CHILLAX, WE'RE LEAVING...
...ONCE THEY COME TO THEIR SENSES.
COME ON, DUDES!
YOU NEVER GO WITH MY PICK!
I NEED MY PROTEIN!
SIGH.
IT'S NOT EASY FOR A MODERN GOTH GIRL TO LIVE WITH SUCH A LIVELY FAMILY.

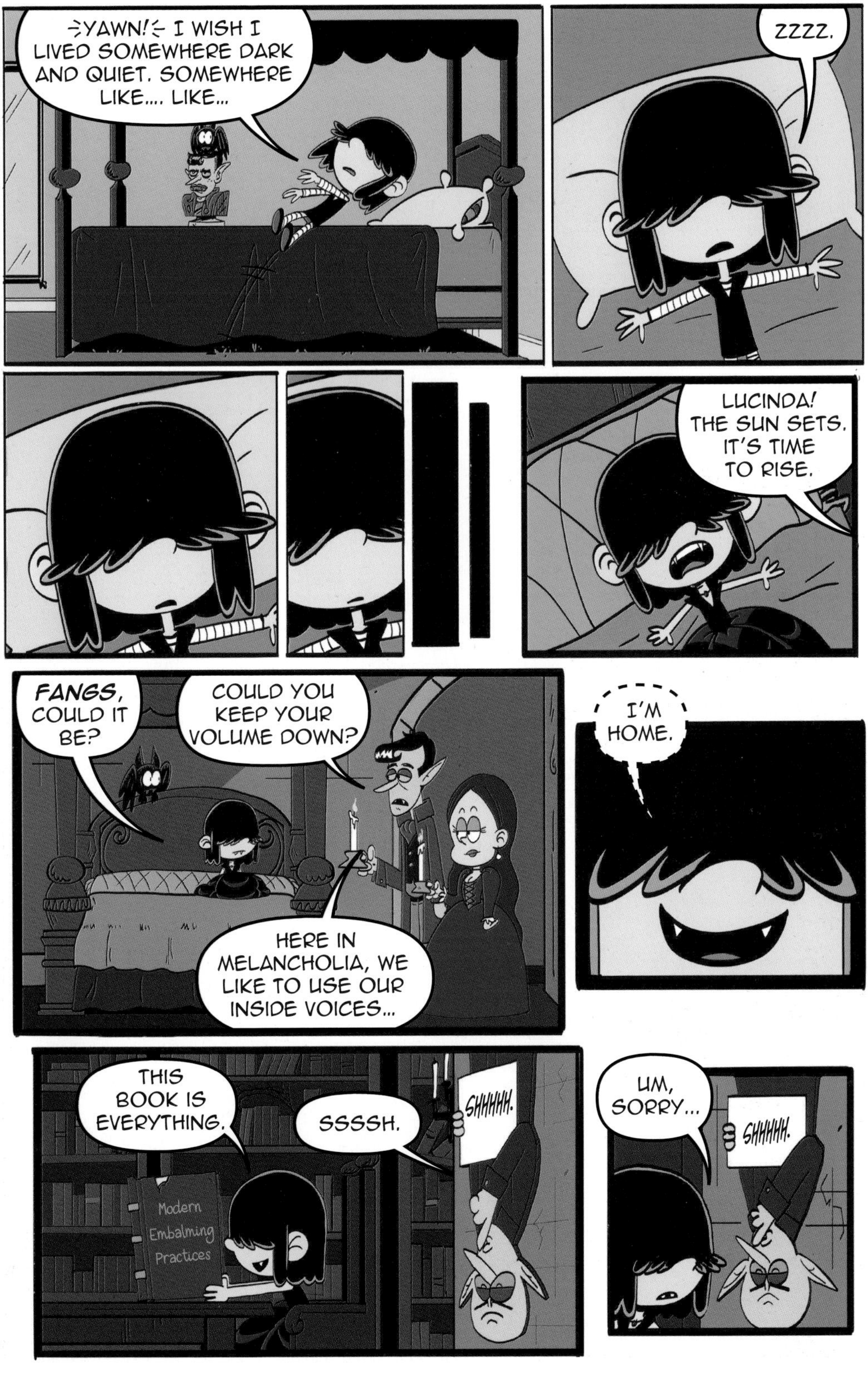

⇉YAWN!⇇ I WISH I LIVED SOMEWHERE DARK AND QUIET. SOMEWHERE LIKE.... LIKE...
ZZZZ.
LUCINDA! THE SUN SETS. IT'S TIME TO RISE.
FANGS, COULD IT BE?
COULD YOU KEEP YOUR VOLUME DOWN?
HERE IN MELANCHOLIA, WE LIKE TO USE OUR INSIDE VOICES...
I'M HOME.
THIS BOOK IS EVERYTHING.
Modern Embalming Practices
SSSSH.
SHHHHH.
UM, SORRY...
SHHHHH.

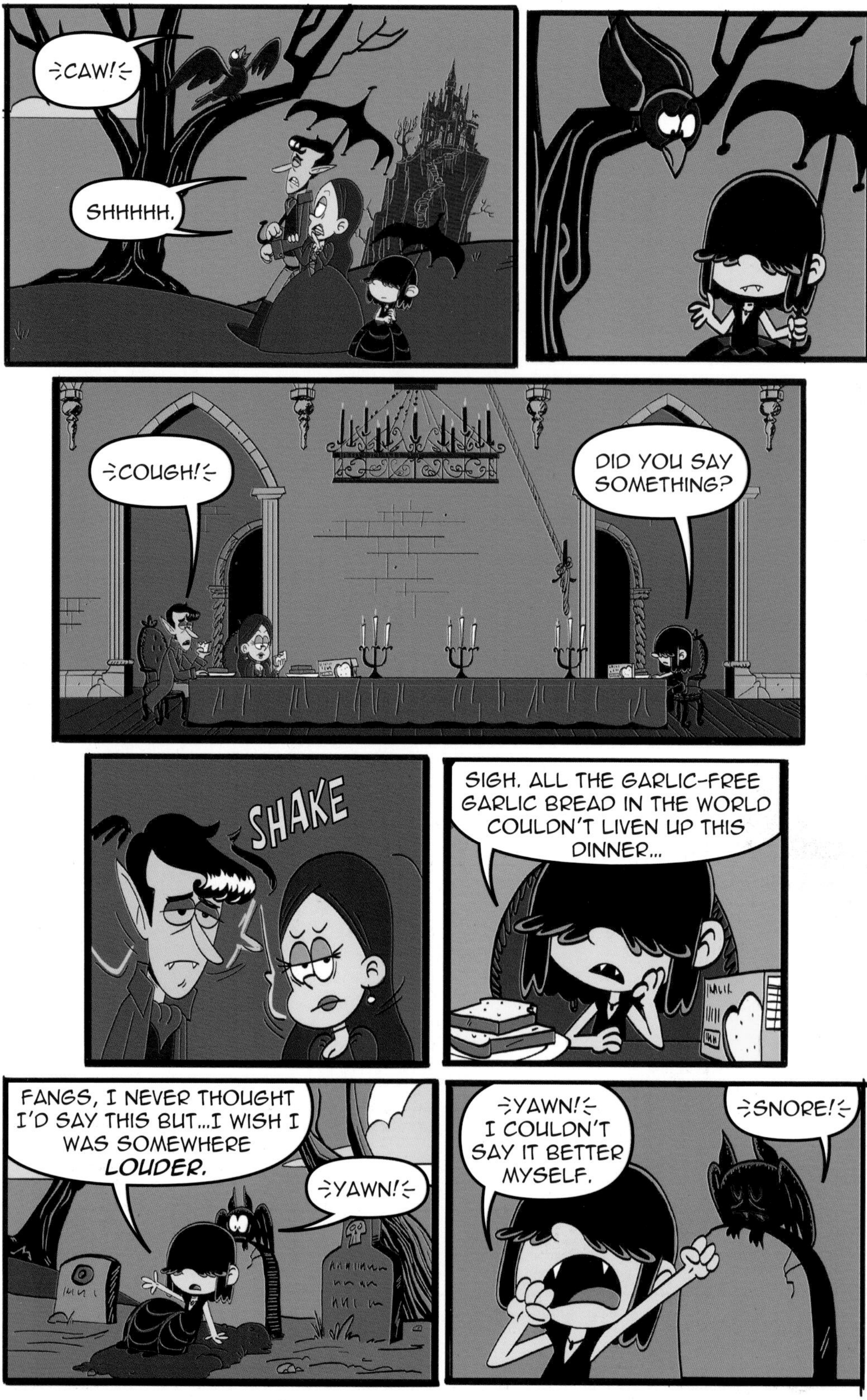

CAW!
SHHHHH.
COUGH!
DID YOU SAY SOMETHING?
SHAKE
SIGH. ALL THE GARLIC-FREE GARLIC BREAD IN THE WORLD COULDN'T LIVEN UP THIS DINNER...
FANGS, I NEVER THOUGHT I'D SAY THIS BUT...I WISH I WAS SOMEWHERE LOUDER.
YAWN!
YAWN! I COULDN'T SAY IT BETTER MYSELF.
SNORE!

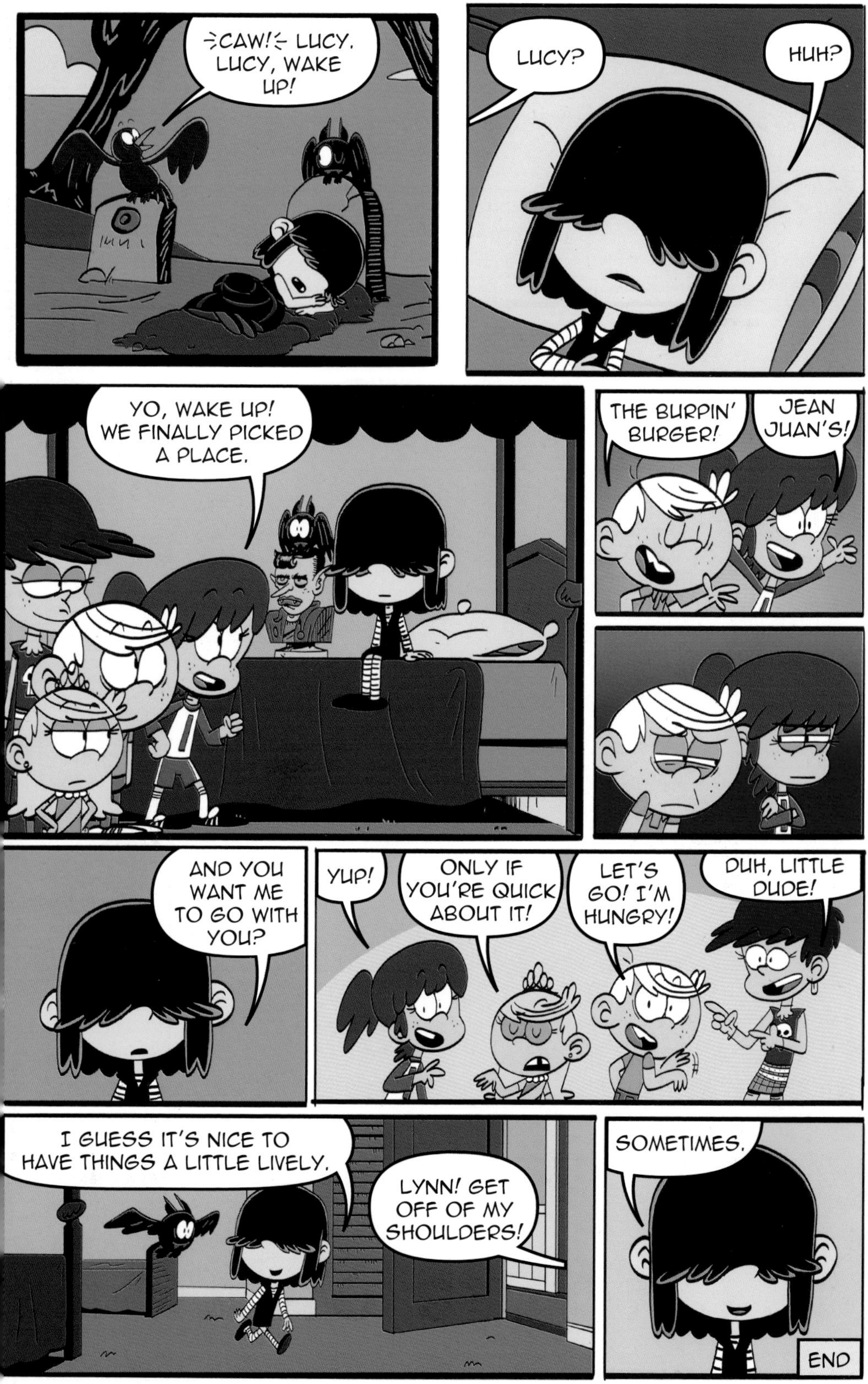
CAW! LUCY. LUCY, WAKE UP!
LUCY?
HUH?
YO, WAKE UP! WE FINALLY PICKED A PLACE.
THE BURPIN' BURGER!
JEAN JUAN'S!
AND YOU WANT ME TO GO WITH YOU?
YUP!
ONLY IF YOU'RE QUICK ABOUT IT!
LET'S GO! I'M HUNGRY!
DUH, LITTLE DUDE!
I GUESS IT'S NICE TO HAVE THINGS A LITTLE LIVELY.
LYNN! GET OFF OF MY SHOULDERS!
SOMETIMES.
END

"Rockin' Routine" by Kiernan Sjursen-Lien – Writer; Lee-Roy Lahey – Artist; Hallie Lal – Colorist; Wilson Ramos Jr. – Letterer

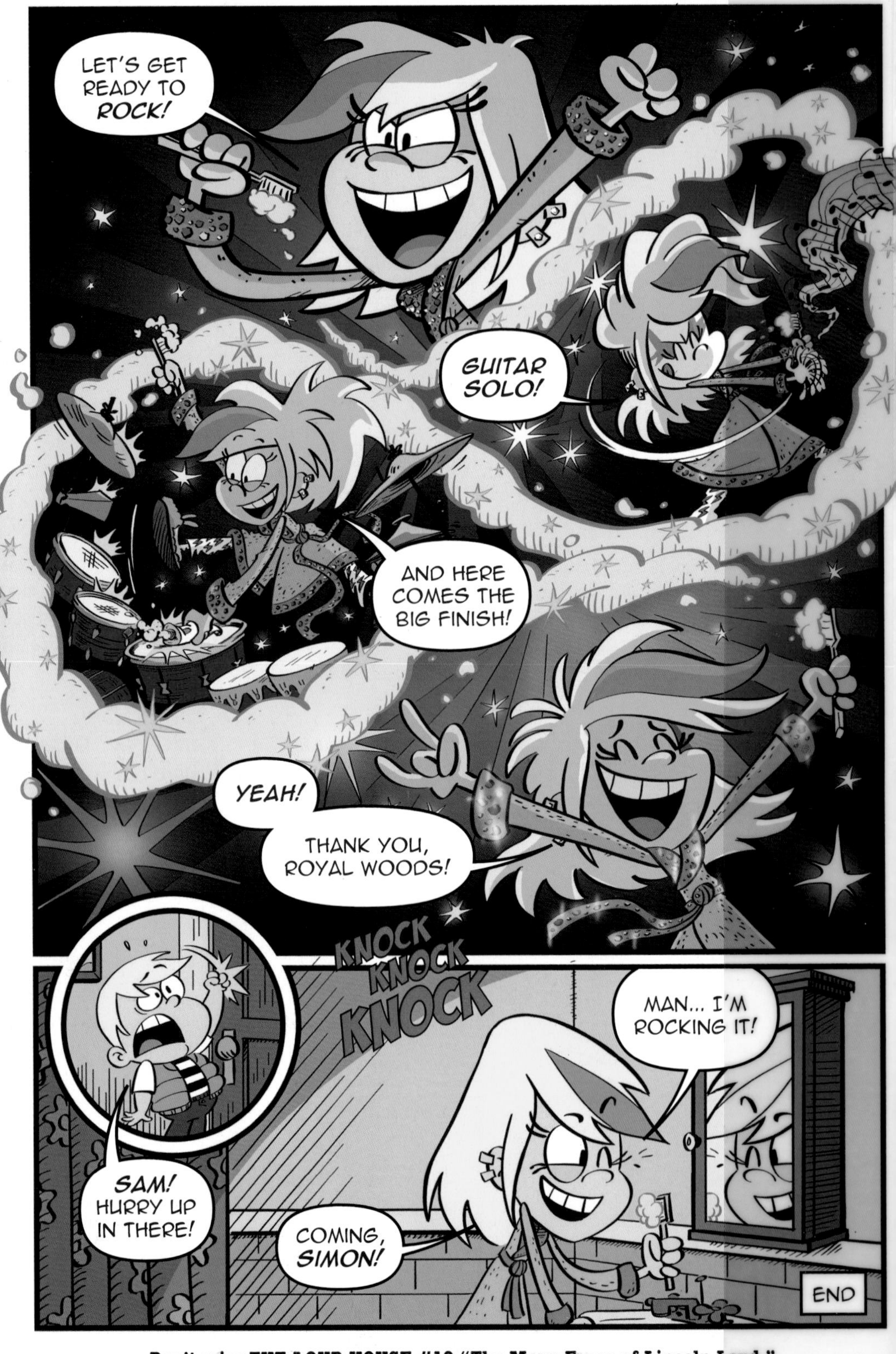
LET'S GET READY TO ROCK!
GUITAR SOLO!
AND HERE COMES THE BIG FINISH!
YEAH!
THANK YOU, ROYAL WOODS!
KNOCK KNOCK KNOCK
SAM! HURRY UP IN THERE!
MAN... I'M ROCKING IT!
COMING, SIMON!
END

Don't miss **THE LOUD HOUSE #10 "The Many Faces of Lincoln Loud,"** available now at booksellers and libraries everywhere!